FIGHTER'S BEST FRIEND

A. RIVERS

Cover design by Steamy Designs

Editing by Free Bird Editing and Paper Poppy Editorial

Sensitivity editing by A Book a Day author services

To Serena,
For making me so much better.

1

SYDNEY

He's not coming.

I'm starving, and exhausted from a twelve-hour shift at the hospital. The mouthwatering aroma of Italian cuisine surrounds me, but I've held off for fifty-eight minutes, waiting for Gabe to show up. At this point, I'm pretty sure he won't. It's not the first time he's become caught up in training and forgotten about me. Probably won't be the last, either. But I'll give him two more minutes. Maybe he'll text or call to say he can't make it. That's not too much to ask, surely?

My phone pings. Heart in my throat, I glance down, but it's Lena. My stomach plummets. I like Lena perfectly fine. In fact, she's one of my closest friends these days, but she isn't Gabe. Moreover, she has a man who's crazy about her, which only serves to remind me that I'm being stood up by the only man in my life. Again. And yeah, technically Gabe is my best friend and not my boyfriend, but we've known each other for most of our lives and have always been closer than many people are comfortable with. Deep down, I'm a little bit in love with him. Not that I'll ever admit as much.

Gabe trains out of the same MMA gym as Lena's boyfriend, Jase, and they're both professional fighters. But while Lena is apparently—according to her message—eating Mexican takeout and about to have mind-blowing sex, I'm sitting alone in a booth like a pathetic loser, hung up on a guy who barely manages to return my calls anymore. Is it too much to ask for a bit of respect? Or at least to be treated like my time matters? Like *I* matter?

My glumness grows and becomes hotter. More angry. I'm sick of this. Sick of being alone at a restaurant after spending a day in the ER, waiting for someone who might never show. I don't want to be achingly lonely. I dedicate far too much emotional energy to Gabe, and just-a-friend or not, I deserve more than that. There was a time when he'd do anything for me. Hell, the first time we met, he saved me from a bully who was pulling on my braids. But our relationship doesn't go two ways anymore. It's always me giving and him taking. How much longer until I have nothing left to give?

I summon the waiter, Marcel, who gives me a sympathetic look. "Can I get the pumpkin ravioli to go, please?"

"No problem, Syd." He makes a note, then asks, "I take it Gabe is a no-show?"

"Seems that way."

He pats my shoulder. "Sorry, sweetheart."

This isn't the first time Marcel and I have had this talk. It's not even the first time this month. Moretti's is a favorite place for Gabe and me to eat, but lately I've been studying the checkered wallpaper and chatting with the staff more than eating.

Scrubbing a hand over my carefully restrained hair, I close my eyes and picture the future stretching out before me, a series of evenings spent by myself, slowly becoming more bitter and disappointed by life. God, I don't want that. I'm only twenty-six, I should be out partying and kissing dozens of frogs before I find my Mr. Right.

I can't let things carry on this way, but if I don't get over my fixation with Gabe, nothing will ever change. I need to let him go and go after what I want: a person who will *always* be there for me. Always put me first. Never leave me waiting and wondering.

Checking my phone, I see he's an hour and five minutes late. As soon as my food comes, I'm out of here. I'm not even going to text to remind him he missed out. I'm tired of his stumbling apologies and complete lack of awareness of my feelings. I love him, but enough is enough.

The restaurant door opens, and a cold breeze blows through. I glance up. There he is. All six feet three inches and 200 pounds of Gabriel Mendoza. He's not smiling—he rarely does—but his eyes crinkle at the corners when they land on me. I don't smile back, even though he steals my breath. It's unfair how hot he is, with thick, dark hair, melting brown eyes and golden skin, courtesy of his Argentinian parents. Some would call his face brutal, with sharp cheekbones and a nose that's been broken more than once, but to me, it's fascinating.

"Sorry I'm late," he says, sliding into the seat opposite me. "You ready to order?"

That's it?

He's over an hour late, and all I get is one half-ass "sorry"?

3

No, I don't think so. I deserve better than his casual thoughtlessness.

"I've already ordered," I tell him. "For myself. Takeout." In case he's unclear about how pissed I am, I add, "You're an hour late."

He winces. "Yeah, sorry about that. The Ruby Knuckles fight is coming up in a few weeks and I needed to get in some extra rounds on the pads."

The Ruby Knuckles event is a big deal for Gabe. He'll face off against Leo "The Lion" Delaney, another scion of boxing royalty. But the opponent isn't what makes it so important. The Ruby Knuckles is an elite mixed martial arts elimination tournament, and it famously marked the end of Gabe's dad's career when he was knocked out in the last round of the finals. Gabe is determined to win where his dad—now manager— failed. He's defeated five other fighters to get to the finals, and now he's really feeling the pressure. I get that. But as far as I'm concerned, it's no excuse not to take twenty seconds to send me a message.

I cock my head. "So Seth asked you to stay later?"

Seth Isles is his coach, and the owner of Crown MMA Gym, where he trains. It's one of the best martial arts gyms in Las Vegas, if not the best.

"Uh, no. He didn't." He scratches the back of his neck. "Dad did."

"Gabe."

He holds up a hand. "I know, I know. Seth is in charge of training. Dad is supposed to butt out and manage the other stuff, but you know how he is. I couldn't say no. I'm here now though, and I'm hungry as fuck."

A sharp pain pricks my heart. I understand how hard it is to let a parent down—I feel like my life is one great big let-down to my mom—but does he actually think so little of me that it didn't cross his mind to, say, get his dad to text me while he was busy training? And does he not see how unacceptable that is? If he respected my time and feelings at all, I'd be at home in bed. My stomach growls, cuing my anger higher.

Oblivious to my hurt, he continues, "Give me a minute to order and we can take it back to your place."

I stand. "You know what? Don't bother. I had a busy shift, I'm tired, and I just want to go home."

He stands, too. "We could watch a movie and blob out on the couch."

I shake my head. He isn't getting it. "Gabe," I say, heart heavy, "I just want to be alone."

GABE

Dread creeps up my spine. Sydney never wants to be alone. She lives for contact with people—both physical and emotional. It's what makes her such a great doctor —well, that and her brilliant mind. Something is seriously wrong. Perhaps something happened at work today. She's in an emergency room rotation, and it can't be easy seeing some of the things she does.

"Bad day at work?" I ask.

"You're *an hour* late," she repeats through clenched teeth.

Uh-oh. This isn't good. Her attitude is directed straight at me, but I'm not sure exactly why she's reacting this way. I mean, yeah I'm late, but I've been late before. I have the fight of my life coming up, and time gets away from me. Usually, if I tell her I'm sorry and offer food or to spend time with her, she doesn't

5

make a big deal of it. But I can tell from the stubborn set of her mouth that she's willing to make a fuss this time.

"You're angry." I state the obvious.

"No shit, Sherlock." She sighs and runs a hand over her tightly-bound black curls. "I just can't do this tonight. I need some time alone."

"You want to be alone," I repeat dumbly. Something feels different about this. Different and *wrong*. Like if I don't say what she wants to hear, I could be in trouble. I don't know how to handle her when she's like this. She's typically so easygoing and eager to hang out that I'm confused and wary of what to do or say next. Should I try to sweet talk her so she comes around? I'm not really a sweet guy, but I can give it a try.

"What about if I buy us dessert on the way to your place?" I suggest. "That brownie you love from the cafe near your apartment?"

She just looks at me, her dark features solemn. "They'll be closed. So no, thank you. I'm not in the mood, anyway."

I wince. From Sydney, this is practically a slap in the face. She doesn't know how to be mean, but she's being distant and snarky, and that's almost worse. She's supposed to be my best friend. The person I get to see once or twice a week, and who always, *always* makes me feel better and brings a smile to my face. She's the person I most look forward to seeing. Now I deflate, beginning to realize I'm not going to get my dose of Sydney today.

Marcel arrives, and hands her a package that smells amazing. He sends me a look, and it's not friendly. "That all, sweetheart?"

"Yes, thanks, Marcel." Without a word to me, she pays him and heads to the exit. I follow, both because

I'm not willing to let her leave without talking this through, and because the neighborhood around her apartment isn't the best and I need to make sure she gets home safely.

Outside, she whirls to face me. "What are you doing?"

Shrugging, I shove my hands in my hoodie pocket. "Walking you home."

"No, you're not." She clutches her takeout to her middle like it's a guard between us. Man, I hate that. Since when has she needed protection from me? "I already told you—"

"I'm just keeping you safe, Syd."

To my astonishment, she rolls her eyes. Usually a statement like that would have earned a soft smile.

"I don't need a guard."

She continues walking, and I fall into step beside her. She speeds up, but despite her sensible work shoes, her legs are significantly shorter than mine and there's no way she can out-pace me. She's determined though, so I drop back and slink along behind her like a fucking stalker because she clearly doesn't want me next to her.

My gaze falls onto her lush, rounded ass. Bad mistake. There isn't much I wouldn't do to grab fistfuls of that butt. Except hurt her. And therein lies the reason I haven't made a move on her in many wonderfully torturous years of being friends—I *would* hurt her. It would just be a matter of when.

My dick stirs in my pants. It likes Sydney's curves a little too much. I've fantasized about running one hand over her lush hips while gripping her ebony hair in my other hand and kissing a path down the column of her throat. Tearing my attention from her ass, I toss a nasty scowl at a guy in a stylish jacket who looks at

7

her for too damn long. He glances away rapidly. Wimp.

I dog her footsteps all the way to her apartment building, giving myself permission to be fascinated by the tendril of hair that caresses the bronze skin of her shoulder.

When we arrive, she gives me the first hint she knows or cares I'm there, calling over her shoulder, "I'm safe, you can go now."

Isn't she going to invite me in? I'd been sure she'd cool off and change her mind on the way over. Sydney doesn't have a temper, which means I was right: something is seriously wrong. I'm beginning to think I've screwed up. I should have tried harder not to be late. Even if I couldn't take a break because Dad was spurring me on from the sidelines, I should have got Jase or Devon—my training buddies and the closest thing I have to brothers—to send her a text. But surely she isn't like this just because I was running behind for dinner?

"Syd..." I trail off when she doesn't look around. "I'm sorry."

"Yeah? Well, so am I." With that, she enters the building and shuts the door behind her. The click of the lock is soft but it echoes like a gunshot in the night. Like a fucking moron, I stare at the door for a good long moment before processing what it means. She's angry at me, and I won't be seeing any more of her tonight. Brooding over what to do next, not accustomed to being cut off like this, I backtrack to the diner and approach Marcel.

"Gabe," he mutters when he sees me.

"Did something bad happen to Syd?" I demand, desperate to understand what's going on, and furious at

8

the thought of anything upsetting her. "Was someone rude or unpleasant to her?"

Marcel rests his forearms on the counter and looks me in the eye. He's one of the few people who's not afraid to do that, because he's known me since I was a kid. "Nothing happened," he says. "Except that she sat there for an hour looking miserable and lonely." He shakes his head. "You're a good guy, but I'm sick of seeing her wait on you. A girl like that should be cherished."

Cherished? Yeah, she fucking should be. But not by me.

"We're not a couple."

Marcel raises a brow. "If you want it to stay that way, you're going about things right."

2

During the Uber ride home from the hospital the next day, I call Lena.

"Girl," I say when she answers. "You, me, wine, and internet dating. My place, in an hour. Interested?"

She laughs. "Provided the internet dating part of that equation is for you and not me, I'm totally in."

I grin. "Like I'd suggest anything else. We both know Jase would tear apart any guy stupid enough to hit on you." Something I try not to be bitter about, but deep down, I want a guy who loves me with that level of ferocity.

"He absolutely would." She sighs dreamily, and I wonder what it says about me that I also envy the fact that everything Jase says and does turns her on. I want a man to press all of my buttons like that—a man who isn't Gabriel Mendoza. "Need me to bring anything?"

I take a moment to reply, mentally running through the contents of my pantry. "Do you have any fancy cheese? I feel like it's a wine and cheese type of night."

"If I don't, I'll get some from a deli on the way over. See you soon." She hangs up, and shortly after, the Uber arrives at my apartment building. I take the stairs to the fourth floor—my exercise for the day—and let myself in. My apartment is modest, with one bedroom, a cramped bathroom, and an open concept area that serves as kitchen, dining and living room combined, but it's the best I can afford considering my hefty student debt. Gabe has offered to pay off my loans a time or two, but I can't let him do that. It would tip the balance of power between us. We've always been equals in our friendship, and I don't want that to change. Besides, I'm content where I am. My place is warm and cozy. I've done my best to make it homey over the years, and all that's missing is a person to snuggle on the sofa with me at the end of a long shift.

I change into pajamas, then let my hair down, and sit while I rub my sore feet. Standing all day really takes a toll on them. Once they're feeling marginally better, I head for the kitchen and put a pizza in the oven. Some days I'm a health nut—it's hard not to be when, as a surgical resident, I see what happens to people with unhealthy lifestyles every day—but right now, I need comfort food.

By the time Lena arrives, I've eaten a couple of slices of pizza, poured us both glasses of wine, and connected my laptop to the television screen, so we have a clear view of the Match-Me homepage. I've created an account, and now it's just waiting for me to input information into my profile. Hearing a knock, I go to the door to let her in.

"Hey, Lee." She's carrying a cheese board to go with the deli bag tucked beneath her arm.

"Hi, Syd." She leans over the board and kisses my cheek. I kiss hers in response.

"I have us all set up in the living room," I say. "Let me take that."

She holds the board out of reach. "Oh, no you don't. You make a start on the wine and I'll just be a moment."

"If you insist." Winking, I go to the sofa and sip wine until she joins me and places the cheeses and a selection of crackers on the coffee table.

"Match-Me," she says, looking up at the screen. "Good choice. Not too stuffy, not too sleazy." She nibbles on a piece of cheese with some kind of seeds or spice in it. "So, you're actually doing this?"

"Did you think I wasn't serious?" That's kind of insulting. "I want a partner. Like what you have with Jase."

She shrugs. "I thought Gabe would get his head out of his ass and officially ask you out. It's obvious he cares for you."

Stuffing a piece of cheese in my mouth, I make an effort not to say the first sarcastic thing that comes to mind. "Someone who cared about me wouldn't let me sit alone at a diner for an hour without so much as a text."

She winces. "He's easily distracted. They all are. You know that. But especially with the Ruby Knuckles final happening soon."

"I know," I agree, loading up a cracker with camembert. "MMA comes first, and it always will until he's proved whatever it is that he thinks he needs to. God knows how long that will take—if he ever gets there. After the Ruby Knuckles, it'll be something else. Tomas has big dreams for him, which is why I've decided to stop waiting."

"Fair enough." She winds an arm around my waist and hugs me. "You deserve to be happy, and you shouldn't accept anything less than what you want. So, let's put your best foot forward." Letting me go, she turns her attention to the empty profile. "Describe yourself," she murmurs. "Hmm. Too easy." She taps away on the keyboard. "Super smart surgeon-in-training with curves for days and the best laugh ever."

I swat at her. "You can't put that!"

"Why not?"

"Because..." I gesture uselessly, then laugh. "It sounds conceited."

"True." With a few keystrokes, she amends the description. "How's that?"

"Better," I allow.

She moves on to the next section. I'm glad she's taken control. I knew she would, which is one of the reasons I invited her over. With Lena here, I won't wimp out.

"What traits do you find attractive in a man?" she asks.

"Physically, or personality-wise?"

"Both."

"Erm..." I turn the question over in my mind. It's not something I've considered much before. I don't really have a type, I just feel a spark around some men and not others. "I'm not fussy," I say. "But he needs to take care of himself. I don't care if he's in amazing shape, but I'm not dealing with someone else's poor lifestyle choices down the road."

"Fair call." She adds a note in the box. "What else?"

Closing my eyes, I try to picture each of the men I've crushed on over the years, but Gabe is the only one who keeps popping into my head, eclipsing them all. "I guess

13

I prefer tall guys. And ones who aren't put off by intelligent, ambitious women."

"Rock solid ego," Lena mutters. "Preferably six feet plus."

I'm on a roll now. "He needs to be kind and supportive."

"Profession?"

I shrug. "Don't care as long as it's legal and he covers his own bills. I'm not being someone's sugar mama. I have enough debt of my own."

"No freeloaders," she says while she types, then sits back. "Okay, I think we've got enough to start with." She turns, wearing a grin. "Time to start searching for the future Mr. Sydney Coleman."

GABE

More than thirty-six hours have passed since our dinner that went nowhere, and I still haven't heard from Sydney. It's weirding me out. Perhaps it makes me needy, but I'm used to hearing from her every few hours, even if I'm too busy to respond. And yeah, I know that makes me sound like an asshole. The thing is, she's my rock. The one consistently good thing in my life. And just seeing her name light up my phone is enough to improve my mood.

Surely she should have cooled down by now and reached out to schedule another get-together. That's what she does. She's a connector. She needs people around, especially ones she's comfortable with. Ones like me. What does it mean that I haven't heard so much as a whisper?

All I know is, it can't be good. She's never shut me out like this before.

I've already tried calling three times since Sunday, and she never picks up. How many calls will it take before I enter crazy stalker territory? Because I have to say, it doesn't feel good. During a break in training, I try again, and leave a voicemail.

"Hey, Syd. It's me. I miss you. Call me."

God, I'm pathetic. If a girl left a message like that on my phone, I'd delete it and never call her back. But this isn't any old girl. It's Sydney. My best friend. My one fucking constant. So I do what any good best friend does, and send her a text.

Gabe: *Want to hang out tonight?*

Okay, I feel lame as soon as I send it, but a guy's gotta do what a guy's gotta do.

"Bro, are you waiting for a call from your dad or something?" Devon, my training buddy, asks as he drops into a seat beside me.

"Sydney," I grunt, shutting the phone off so he can't see that this isn't the first text I've sent without a reply. He may be one of my best friends, but he'd be merciless if he knew how desperate I am for a response. Sydney gets me out of my head. Devon and Jase, much as they mean well, only push me deeper into it, because MMA consumes their thoughts as well as mine. It's our shared addiction. I need Sydney to bring everything back into perspective.

My phone buzzes and I jump, scrambling to open it. Devon's eyes widen. I scan the text.

Sydney: *I have plans.*

That's it. No details. No offer of a rain check. Just those three words.

"Ouch." Devon winces. "Sorry, man." Ignoring him, I type back, *I'll make time whenever suits you. As long as it's not during training.*

"Hey, Jase, come over here!" Devon waves our other training buddy over, and I scowl at him in warning. I can already see he's planning something, and I won't like it. "You know anything about what Sydney is up to tonight that she'd blow off Gabe for?"

Jase shrugs one tattooed shoulder as he crosses to us. "Beats me, but I think Lena is going over to her place after work."

Lena LaFontaine is Jase's girlfriend. The newest member of our circle. A possibility occurs to me: is Sydney replacing me with a girl best friend? Lots of people say our friendship is unconventional, but she's never seemed to mind that before. Perhaps with Lena around, things have changed.

The phone buzzes.

Sydney: *Maybe in a couple days.*

Frustrated, I drop it and run a hand through my hair. Hardly anything riles me, but she's always been the key to unlocking my hotter emotions, and right now I want to hunt her down, shake her, and demand to know what's going on.

Finally, I look up at Jase. From here, he towers over me, but if I stood, I'd be a couple inches taller than him. "Has Lena said what they've been doing together?"

There's a gleam in his eye. One I don't like.

"She's experimenting with online dating. They set up an account for her yesterday and I think they're getting together tonight to look over the candidates."

I shoot to my feet. "What. The. *Fuck*." Crossing my arms over my chest, I look down at him. "You'd better be fucking kidding me."

He grins, his expression sly. "Can't say I am."

I mutter every Spanish curse word in my vocabulary, knowing Jase and Devon won't understand a word of it. *Hell.* She's blowing me off to browse for men online like she's picking a date from a shopping catalog? Talk about insulting. Not to mention, why does she think she needs to go fishing for men online? She's beautiful, and damned smart. With her killer figure and flawless complexion, she could have any guy she wanted, any time she wanted him. Do you know what kind of men approach women online? Predators, that's who.

"She can't do that," I snap, knowing I sound crazy but unable to switch it off. She's had this effect on me since I was twenty years old and barged into her dorm room while she was getting it on with some French douche from her anatomy class. I'd never been attracted to her before then, but ever since, images of her curvy, perfect body have tormented me. She's the full package. And even though I can't have her and I've always intended to step aside when she meets the right guy, I know that any bottom-feeder who thinks a dick pic is the key to her heart won't be worthy of her.

"Does she know how many dangerous men are online?" I ask, stomping past Jase to unleash an almighty kick on one of the heavy bags. "They'll look at her and see easy pickings. Hell no, this is not okay."

I'll find a way to stop her. I have to. For her own safety, not because I'm a jealous asshole.

Devon chortles. "Good luck breaking the news to her. Don't know if you've noticed, but women don't like being told what to do. Sydney has a mind of her own."

"Don't care." I kick the bag again, and the thud is deeply satisfying. Especially when I can imagine I'm striking a faceless bastard who wants to get his hands on my Sydney. "She's not doing it."

My friends exchange a look, but I ignore them. They don't know Sydney the way I do. I can talk her out of this. I can talk her out of anything.

Right?

3

SYDNEY

"What about this guy?" Lena opens a message from a guy named Jordan that says, *Hey beautiful, want to get coffee?*

It isn't witty, but it's also far less vulgar than some of the others I've received. The number of men who send lewd comments under the guise of jokes is outrageous. At least the ones who send dick pics are upfront about what they want and give me the chance to check out their goods, so to speak.

"Show me more," I say, and she clicks on his profile. His photo fills the screen. Jordan is a handsome black man with a great smile and an adorable golden retriever. "Ooh, nice. He passes the first test."

"He enjoys comedy shows, basketball, and long walks in the park with his best friend, Frankie," Lena says in her television presenter voice. "That's sweet. Do we like him?"

I study the short lines of text, wishing there was some way I could cut through the image he's projecting and get right down to what he's actually like. But if that ability existed, far fewer people would be divorced.

"He sounds nice." Even to my own ears, I sound hesitant. "Yeah," I add more confidently. "We like him."

"Fantastic." Lena navigates back to the messages and types in, *Tomorrow?*

I'm so glad she's doing the hard work because I'd chicken out before hitting send whereas she doesn't waver for a moment. I suppose it's easier to be that way when it's not her romantic life on the line. Two minutes later, I have a coffee date scheduled during my lunch hour tomorrow.

"Thanks, babe." I high-five Lena, then return my attention to the next guy in my inbox. Even without clicking into the conversation, I can see the head of a penis staring at me. "Hard pass."

Lena laughs. "Ruthless. Was it the bush?"

"Nah, I don't mind a little hair, but common decency is a strict requirement."

She moves on to the next guy. "How about Dean? He wants to know if you're interested in getting drinks this week?"

Frowning, I purse my lips. "Is 'drinks' code for sex? I'm so out of touch with the dating scene."

Lena winks. "Not if you say no. Is that a yes to Dean?"

I gesture at the screen. "Gimme."

Dean is average height, white, and built like a tank. His profile displays a number of photos of him flexing his biceps.

"Nope," I say. "Too self-centered."

My phone buzzes on the cushion beside us and I reach for it, checking the caller ID. It's Gabe. I reject the call. My anger from the weekend has faded, but I'm still not ready to talk to him.

"You know, you should probably get that," Lena says, reading the name over my shoulder. "He's just going to keep calling. Jase says he's a nightmare at the gym, and if you keep putting him off, he'll get all broody and sulky."

"Gabe?" I snort. "Could he get any broodier?"

She rolls her eyes. "You know what I mean. Men are so damn annoying when they're pouty."

"True, that." The phone rings again, and I almost answer. Then I remember how it felt to sit by myself at the diner, lonely and pitiful. "Screw him. If he wants to see me, he can turn up next time we make plans."

"Fair call."

Dismissing the phone, I take over the computer controls and find a guy who looks promising. "Nathan," I say to myself. "You just scored yourself a date."

My phone vibrates with a text. I'd happily delete it straight away—although I'd feel guilty for it later—but Lena reads it aloud before I have the chance.

"Gabe wants to know if he can come over."

"Tell him I'm busy with you."

She props her hands on her hips. "You know, I'm all for this independence and dating thing, but avoidance isn't my style. If you want to blow him off, you can do it yourself."

"Fine." Taking the phone, I do just that. Then I shut it off and do my best to put my hot MMA-fighting best friend to the back of my mind.

"ARE you sure it's not too much?" I ask Hayley, one of the nurses I work with, as I adjust the belt around my waist. I've ditched my scrubs for a purple dress with a flirty skirt that hits mid-thigh, because no one thinks scrubs are sexy—at least, not on women.

Hayley puts her hands on my shoulders and directs me to the mirror. "Syd, you look gorgeous. The guy is going to eat his tongue when he sees you."

I wince. "That sounds painful."

Laughing, she releases me. "Not literally. Although I'm sure you'd know how to help him if he did." She hands me a tube of lipstick and I check the color. It's deep maroon, not a choice I'd typically make, but I swipe it over my lips and can't help but be impressed by the effect.

"Gorgeous," she repeats. "Now go find your date, and get lucky on behalf of all of us who work too many hours to have a life."

With a parting smile, I leave the changing room and head for the cafeteria, where I'm meeting Jordan for lunch. Unfortunately, I need to be nearby during my break in case any emergencies arise, but hopefully he'll understand, and the cafeteria food really isn't that bad. Scanning the room, I spot him in a far corner, seated at one of the tables that's often abandoned. He looks just like he did in his photographs. Hot. *Really* hot.

Then why aren't I more excited to see him?

He looks up and gives me the blinding smile I recognize from the internet.

Do I flutter? No. No, I do not.

Something is terribly wrong with me. This is a prime specimen of a man I'm approaching, and all I can think is that it feels like I'm sneaking around behind Gabe's back. It's ridiculous, considering we aren't dating and never have. Heck, the most action I've received from him was the time he got sloppy drunk at his twenty-first birthday and slipped as he tried to kiss my cheek, landing on my chin just south of my mouth instead. He's never even tried to cop a feel. Both Jase and Devon have done that much at least. Gabe Mendoza is very bad for my ego, and worse for my peace of mind. But I won't let him ruin this date.

Plastering a smile across my face, I sit opposite Jordan. "Hi, I'm Sydney. It's lovely to meet you."

"Back at you, Sydney." He flashes his pearly whites. "So, you're a doctor?"

"A surgical resident," I correct. "Sorry about the venue. I couldn't get away from work today."

"No problem." His deep brown eyes warm as they scan my face. "I'd rather eat here than wait another day to see you."

Aww, now that's sweet. Exactly the sort of thing that should melt my heart. But no melting occurs because the thing is, this guy isn't Gabe—who is apparently the only person I want to hear those words from. Damn it.

"Thank you. Have you eaten?"

"No, I thought I'd wait until you arrived and order us both a sandwich, if that works for you."

"That sounds great." It saves me from ordering a salad and fighting off hunger pangs later. "I'll have chicken on rye, please."

"Coming right up."

As Jordan gets our food, my phone buzzes, and I take the opportunity to check it while he's gone. Something tells me it's Gabe. After constantly being difficult to get in touch with, all of a sudden he's blowing up my phone. Typical, right? Despite my best intentions, I open the message.

Gabe: *Make sure he isn't a serial killer.*

That's it. Nothing else. No opening, no explanation about who he's referring to—although I know anyway. Someone told him about my date today. Lena wouldn't have broken my confidence, but she might have mentioned it to Jase, who would have gladly rubbed Gabe's nose in the fact he knew something his friend didn't. I roll my eyes, but secretly, it is kind of nice to know he's concerned about me.

When Jordan returns, I ask outright, "Are you a serial killer?"

He blinks at me, stunned, then laughs. "No, of course not. Are you?"

A reluctant smile lifts my lips. "No. Sorry, my friend told me to ask."

He offers me a chicken sandwich and picks up his own, which appears to be beef. "Don't worry about it." He takes a bite, chews, and then wipes his mouth on a napkin. "Let me guess: it's been a while since you did this."

Cheeks burning, I nod. "Guilty as charged. If I say anything strange, assume that's why."

He grins, and it really is a nice smile, it just doesn't do anything for me. "I was in your shoes a couple of months ago. I recently got out of a three-year relationship and didn't remember how to do this anymore. It'll come back to you."

"Thanks, you're nice." And I feel nothing for him. For a while, we talk, and he tells me all about his dog—the wonderfully goofy Frankie—and shows me several pictures of the two of them in different poses. Jordan is cute, and easy to talk to, but by the time we part ways, I know there won't be a second date and I suspect he does too.

He kisses my cheek. "Nice meeting you, Sydney. I hope you find what you're looking for."

"Same here, Jordan. Hug Frankie for me."

I return to work, disappointed but not dispirited. Jordan may not have given me butterflies, but there's nothing to say the next guy won't. I just hope he can make me feel as much as my best friend does.

GABE

It's the day after Sydney's lunch date with some asshole she met online—which I had to find out about third-hand—and although she replied to my text to tell me she'd survived unharmed, she didn't respond when I asked how it had gone. Now I have no fucking idea how she is—other than alive—and it's driving me nuts. That's why, as soon as training ends, I race through the shower with the intention of heading to her place. But the moment I'm out, Dad steps in front of me.

The corners of his eyes crinkle and he breaks out in a grin. "You looked good out there today, *mijo*. You keep that up and you'll be in good shape for Leo."

"Thanks. But I need to get through the fight next week first."

"Psh." He waves a hand dismissively. "Like you need to worry about that. So, how about you come by our place and talk tactics?"

Ugh. Can't I catch a break?

"Sorry, Dad. Not tonight. I have plans with Sydney."

I don't like lying to him, but I console myself with the fact that I am actually planning to go over there, even if I don't "have plans" with her per se.

He pulls a face. "Does it have to be tonight? The big fight will arrive before you know it."

God, this is hard. It's not often I deny Dad anything. He's my hero. I grew up watching from the front row while he faced off against some of the MMA and boxing greats. I was also there the night he lost everything and I saw how hard he took it, so I know how badly he wants me to succeed. But there's still plenty of time to get our tactics sorted, and I'm not going to be able to think straight until I assure myself that Sydney and I are okay.

"Yeah, it does. Rain check?"

His lips press together and he's clearly not pleased, but he nods. "Next week."

"Done. *Adios, Papa.* Catch you later."

"Bye, son."

I sling my bag over my shoulder and leave before he can call me back. My motorbike is parked outside and I drive it to her apartment and let myself into the building with the key she had made for me. After the incident when I walked in on her having sex, I always knock at her apartment rather than making myself at home, just to be safe.

The door swings open and Sydney stands in the doorway, fastening a necklace. It's silver, with a cute charm on the end, and falls just to the top of her fabulous tits.

"Gabe?" She seems confused by my presence. "What are you doing here?"

Brushing past her, I make myself at home on her sofa. "I came to talk."

"Oh." She swallows. "Any reason in particular?"

I stare at her. Is she kidding me right now? She's been dodging me for days, and she has no idea why I'm here? I don't buy it. She just wants to make me say the words. I've never been a great talker—a sore spot between us because she's all about maintaining open lines of communication.

"I missed you," I grind out, forcing myself to relax. "So I came to see you."

She brightens. "Well, that's nice." Then her expression falls. "But I'm actually heading out. Sorry."

Out? She's going out? What does that even mean?

"Where to? I'll come with you."

She smiles wryly. "Probably best you don't. I have a date, and I don't think he'll appreciate me bringing another man along, even if he is my best friend."

A date? What the fuck? She's blowing me off to spend time with another guy? One she doesn't even know? A sense of wrongness overwhelms me, and a muscle ticks in my jaw. I turned down my father to be here, and she should be joining me on the sofa to watch a movie and snuggle, not putting on jewelry for someone else.

Flirting with someone else. *Kissing* someone else.

Has she considered her safety?

"Syd, you know it's dangerous to meet people off the internet. Do you really need to take the risk? Aren't you being a bit careless?"

Oh, shit. Immediately, it's obvious I've said the wrong thing. Her nostrils flare, her eyes narrow, and she takes a step toward me.

"I'm going to pretend you didn't say that." Her hands fist at her sides. "Because I know you didn't mean to question my intelligence. I work at a hospital, Gabe. I know full well the dangers of trusting the wrong person, and I promise you, I'm taking precautions."

God, I'm messing all of this up. It's just that, while I always said I'd step aside and let her date someone else

27

when the time came, I don't want it to happen like this. It feels wrong, all the way down to my bones. Things between us are tense, and they shouldn't be. We're supposed to be closer than that. I don't want to lose our friendship. And as far as her dating goes, I always figured she'd meet some guy at the hospital and be swept off her feet—maybe a doctor. But online is a whole other story, and I'm not cool with it.

And fuck it, I just plain don't want anyone else touching her.

"Please, Syd. I'm asking you, as my friend, to cancel this date." She hesitates, and I try to press my advantage. "Isn't our friendship more important than some guy who might turn out to be a psycho?"

"Oh. My. God," she growls through gritted teeth, and I can honestly say I've never heard anything quite like it. "This isn't about pitting you against him." She throws her hands in the air. "It's about me prioritizing myself for once, okay? So deal with it."

Stalking to her bedroom, she shoves the door shut but I catch it and follow her in. "Explain it to me. I want to understand." But I don't get it. I just don't.

Grabbing the hem of her shirt, she whips it off, and my jaw drops. *Mierda*, she's undressing in front of me. What the hell is going on here? And damn, her body is even more gorgeous than I remember. Her back is to me, and the skin is smooth and looks so soft that my fingers twitch at my sides, desperate to touch it. The clasp of a black silk bra meets over her spine, and my cock really likes the look of it. I bet that bra is sheer and lacy around the front, cupping her full tits just perfectly. Wiping a hand over my eyes, I grind my back teeth and try really hard not to think about my best friend's assets.

"I'm going whether you're here or not," she says. "I

28

won't let you make me late." With that, she shoves her pants off and gives me a clear view of her first-rate ass. My heart thumps erratically and threatens to quit. Holy fuck, her panties match her bra and I was right—they're sheer. My throat closes over. I can't breathe. It's all I can do not to grab her rounded hips and yank her back into my erection. I want to rub myself on her. To peel down those panties and do dirty, filthy things to her. It's been too long since I got laid, and she's too beautiful for me to handle.

Then, thank God, she slips a buttery yellow dress over her head and lets it fall into place, covering all of the important parts. But then I get a better look at the dress. It's too pretty. She looks fresh and playful, and I'd much rather she change into a sack. Knowing her, she'd find a way to make that sexy, too.

She grabs a hairbrush and a bunch of pins from the cabinet and wrestles her hair into a messy bun. "All right, Gabe," she says, turning to me. "I'll try to explain." She wrings her hands and I want to grab them and tell her to stop. She's a surgeon, so she can't afford to be so rough on the tools of her trade. "The thing is, I feel like I've become too dependent on you to meet my emotional needs, and that's not fair to either of us."

I don't see why not, but this is clearly difficult for her and it must be important or she wouldn't be putting the both of us through it, so I hold my tongue.

"I need to find someone who's more available for me," she says, and her words cut with the accuracy of a scalpel. She's right; I haven't been around for her lately. I've been consumed by winning the Ruby Knuckles. But even when she's had a stressful day at work, she's always been there for me and I haven't returned the favor.

Fuck, I feel like a shithead.

One of her hands flutters over her chest. "I need that, for my own wellbeing, and I'm going to put my needs first for once. So please don't make this harder than it already is. You know it takes a lot for me to prioritize myself."

"I do." My voice is rough and I feel lower than low. Sydney didn't grow up with much in the way of love or affection. Her parents were distant, which is part of the reason she adopted mine as stand-ins. She deserves all the devotion in the world. I accepted years ago that I can't give that to her, so I ought to get out of her way and let her find it. That doesn't make me want to crack her date across the jaw any less, but the gleam of tears in her eyes fells me more effectively than any opponent ever has.

"Sorry, Syd. I wasn't seeing clearly. You're right." Bending, I kiss her cheek. She smells like antiseptic, and it may be weird, but I love it. "I'll see myself out, but can we spend time together tomorrow?"

"I suppose that would be all right." She smiles hesitantly. "Text me?"

"I will."

She grabs my hands and squeezes. "Thanks, Gabe. I appreciate that."

4

Yesterday's date was a bust. The guy was a jerk, which only made me feel worse about how I'd behaved toward Gabe. In his own style, he'd been trying to help. I feel like we've made up some ground, but we have a long way to go before we get back to normal—if such a thing is even possible. When Gabe texts to set something up, I suggest he comes over to my place because honestly, I'm half-afraid he's going to forget despite making such a fuss about it. I can't handle the thought of sitting in Moretti's waiting for him to turn up again.

But at seven o'clock there's a knock on the door and I answer it to find him standing there in dark jeans and a charcoal-colored shirt with a grocery bag in one hand.

"Hi." I smile tentatively. Things have been weird between us, and while I know that's largely my fault, I'm not going to take back all of the things I've said because I meant every word.

"Hey, Sydney." He bends and brushes a kiss over my cheek. Blood rushes to the surface, the same way it always does when he kisses me, even though it doesn't

31

mean anything. It's just the way he and his family operate, and while he's closed-off with most people, he's affectionate with the few he's close to.

"What's all this?" I gesture at the bag as he enters.

"I'm making you dinner." He drops the bag on the kitchen counter and starts pulling items out. "Grilled vegetables with some of my mama's homemade chimichurri."

"Really?" I lean against the counter and watch as he switches the oven on and takes the cling wrap off a plate of prepared vegetables. Valentina Mendoza's chimichurri is legendary. "That sounds delicious. I can't believe you're cooking."

He gives me a look. Darkly amused. "Least I can do after... you know."

"Do you need help?"

He shakes his head and grabs a baking sheet from the cupboard. He's here at least a couple of times a month so he's familiar with where everything is kept. While he's setting out the vegetables, I open up the container of chimichurri and sniff.

"Smells delicious."

"Of course." His hand movements are precise and assured. I shouldn't expect anything less. That's how he approaches everything in life. He's not outwardly boastful but he has confidence aplenty. I bet he'd touch a woman with the same care. "As if Mama would let me away with anything less." He gets the vegetables in the oven and washes his hands. "Might be forty minutes or so. Want to start a movie?"

"That sounds perfect."

He comes around the counter and pauses at my side, close enough that my stomach flutters in excitement. He's not even touching me, but his scent fills my nostrils and electricity sparks between our bodies. His face is impassive, so maybe I'm the only one feeling it.

Jerking into motion, I cross the room and settle on the sofa. The laptop is on the other cushion so I shift it to my knee and turn on the screen. The Match-Me site lights up and I click out of it before he can see.

"What kind of movie?" I ask, opening Netflix.

He sits beside me and ducks his head close to mine, his arm brushing the bare skin of my shoulder. My breath catches, and I hope he doesn't notice. He shifts closer and is it my imagination, or does he release a soft sigh?

"A comedy?"

"A comedy it is." I select a movie with a couple of goofy guys in police uniforms and prop the laptop on a stool opposite us, then connect it wirelessly to the TV.

The film begins, but I'm more aware of the man beside me than what's happening on the screen. He stretches and slings his arm across the top of the sofa, his fingers dangling down and brushing my shoulder. I shiver.

"Are you cold?" he asks. "Want me to get a blanket?"

"I'm fine." I'm just not sure what to do with this uneasy truce between us. Usually I'd snuggle into his side, but I'm feeling a bit fragile.

"I'll keep you warm." His arm drops down around me and he yanks me into his side. I can feel the bulge of his bicep through my top. "Better?"

"Yeah." I rest my head on his shoulder. It seems like we're doing the cuddling after all.

He chuckles, but I have no idea what's funny. We stay there for a while longer, the smell of grilled vegetables slowly permeating the room from the open plan kitchen. Eventually, he gets up to check them and I pause the movie and join him, then I dish the vegetables while he serves the chimichurri and puts on the finishing touches.

"Honestly, this is going to be the best meal I've had all week," I tell him.

"It doesn't beat Moretti's," he replies hesitantly, eyeing me as if he wants to broach the topic of our spat but doesn't know how to do it.

I shrug. "The company improves the food, and your mama's chimichurri is divine."

A smile curves lips that are far too sensual for a man who fights for a living. "So you... like... the company?"

I return his smile more confidently. "Yes, the company is exactly what I need today."

A full-fledged grin breaks over his face. "Same here. Now, let's eat."

The rest of the night passes in the fashion I'm used to. The tension has broken and we're more comfortable with each other. We eat, watch the movie, and talk. Nothing deep, but the kind of surface stuff that leaves me feeling good about where we can go from here. The only moment that gives me pause is when he asks how my date went last night. I admit it was a bust and he grunts while he tries to figure out what to say. I brush it off with some half-ass comment and five minutes later, we're back in the rhythm of being us. Hopefully it lasts.

GABE

I'm going to see her again tonight. Although everything ended well after our movie session a few days ago, I feel like Sydney and I really need one more night to cement our friendship. Right now, I'm not completely secure in it, and I don't like feeling uncertain where she's concerned. She's supposed to be my constant. Friends come and go, fights come and go, but Sydney is always there. Isn't she?

A horn honks outside, and I check my phone. Sure enough, there's a text from Jase. I lock up and head outside. His Camaro is idling on the curb. Lena is in the front seat, and she waves as I approach. The back seat is clear so I squeeze in, my knees coming up to my chest. It's a reasonably sized car, but my legs don't fit many places well. Airplanes are especially bad, which is why I usually fly first class. Well, that, and who wouldn't, given the option?

"Is it just the five of us tonight?" I ask as Jase pulls back onto the road.

"Yeah. I invited a few guys from the gym to make it an even eight, but they already had plans."

I nod, although I doubt he can see. Bowling is something we like to do together a few times a year. We had four players—Jase, Devon, Sydney, and I—but Lena throws our numbers off. Not that I'm not pleased to have her here. She's a cool girl, and she got Jase out of hot water, which means she has my approval. We stop at Devon's apartment building first, and he sits on the other side, which forces Sydney to squish into the middle when we pick her up. She scoots over my thighs, giving me just enough time to appreciate the soft curves of her ass before she lands in the center and belts up.

"Hey, beautiful," Devon says, wrapping one arm around her.

My eyes narrow, and I shoot a glare over her head. The guys know better than to touch Sydney around me. She's off-limits. But that doesn't stop Devon from trying to rile me up.

35

"Hi, Dev." She smiles up at him but doesn't relax into his body the way she does mine, and satisfaction fists in my gut. Maybe it's masochistic to notice these things, but I can't help it. She's my addiction. And if I can't touch her the way I want, then the second best thing is to hold onto that special place she carved out for me in her heart when we were kids. I've never come close to losing it before, and I don't intend to now.

"I hear you've been looking for a man," Devon says, his attention fully on Sydney.

I want to wring his neck, but it's not exactly his fault he's goading me so much. As far as he and Jase know, I'm protective of Sydney because she's my *friend*. Like a *sister*. They don't realize I freak the fuck out when anyone lays their hand on her or flirts with her because she's *mine*. At least, in my head she is. In reality, she'd probably laugh her ass off if I said as much.

Okay, she wouldn't. She's too nice for that. But she knows I can't give her what she wants, and based on how she reacted the other day, she wouldn't hesitate to remind me of that.

"Just starting the search," she replies, her tone tense. She doesn't know how I feel about her, but she senses that her love life makes me a little crazy and probably doesn't want to antagonize me when we're smoothing things over. "I've been on a couple of dates but haven't met anyone I want to go on a second one with yet."

Covering my mouth, I try to hide my relief. Based on her expression, I fail.

"It's a pity Gabe outlawed every guy at the gym, or you'd have plenty to choose from."

Devon seriously has a death wish.

Sydney laughs. "That doesn't bother me. Dating someone from the gym could get messy if it went wrong.

I'm best to keep my romantic life separate from my friends until I meet someone I can see a future with."

"Smart move," Lena says. "Plenty of options online, anyway. No need to go fishing in the gym's pool."

I take Sydney's hand, give it a squeeze, and swallow past the boulder in my throat. "You'll find the right guy. He's out there, and once he finds you, he won't let go."

"Aww." Her expression softens, and emotion shines in her eyes. "Thank you."

Releasing her hand, I set mine firmly on my lap before I do something stupid like raise her palm to my lips and kiss it.

"No problem. It's what you deserve."

In front of us, Lena swats Jase's upper arm. "You need to take some lessons from Gabe. That's how you talk to a woman."

He scowls in the rearview mirror. "Thanks, bro. No need to raise the bar any further."

A moment later, he flicks the turn signal on and the car swerves into the casino's parking garage. He finds a spot and we spill out.

I stretch my cramped limbs and groan. "Next time, I call shotgun."

Jase shakes his head. "Sorry, no can do. My girl gets the front seat."

Lena rolls her eyes. "You can have it. I don't mind. Me and Syd can catch up on girl talk in the back."

"Thanks. Appreciate it."

We head inside. The bowling alley is busy tonight, but there are a few lanes free and after renting shoes, we cross over to one of them and enter our details into the machine. It snaps photos of each of us. Jase looks like a goof, too busy watching Lena bend over to do up her laces to pay attention. Devon strikes a tough-guy pose,

37

and the camera captures Lena mid eye-roll. My photo makes me look like I want to kill someone—which seems to be standard—and Sydney is cute as a fucking button. Because of course she is.

Jase goes first, knocking down an impressive ten pins. Devon has a gutter-ball, and his second only clips the edge. Lena bowls a strike and nods as if she totally expected it. Is she a secret bowling master and no one thought to mention it? I score a respectable nine and then Sydney makes her way up to the lane. She grabs a ball, slips her fingers into it, and adopts an awkward stance. I cross my fingers for her. When it comes to the size of her brain and her manual dexterity, she crushes us all, but sports are another thing entirely. She's never been good at them, and that's understating it.

She takes a deep breath, steels herself, and swings her arm back, then forward. The ball launches into the air, smacks back onto the polished wooden surface, and promptly lurches into the gutter. I wince. Every time we come here I want to believe that I've amplified how bad she is in my mind, and every time she proves me wrong.

"Welp." She throws her hands up. "Guess I didn't magically grow skills since last time."

We all go another round, and Lena comes out on top.

"Who invited her?" Devon asks, tone teasing.

She shrugs. "I don't need an invitation."

"Touché."

On the third go-around, I simply can't bear to watch Sydney earn another zero.

"Let me help."

She shakes her head, cheeks flushed. "There's no saving me, Gabe. You know I'm hopeless. We go through this every time."

"And one day it'll stick."

"Go on, gorgeous," Devon urges. "He can't make it worse."

She narrows her eyes at him and he holds up his hands placatingly.

"You know we love you whether or not you can bowl," he adds.

For once, I might actually owe him. Standing, I approach her and take the ball, demonstrating how it should be done.

She sighs impatiently. "You can show me all you like. It's not going to make a difference."

Frustration sours my mouth. It's just a stupid game, but I hate to hear her admit defeat. "How about we do it together?"

"Okaaaay." She drags the word out dubiously. "How did you plan to do that?"

"Here." I offer her the ball. "Hold it like you normally would."

She slips her fingers into the holes and faces the pins. "Now what?"

Heart in my throat, I approach her from behind and line my body up against hers. My arm follows the line of hers and rests on the back of the ball. The coconutty scent of her hair makes me want to bury my face in it and sniff, but I resist. As it is, the guys can probably see way more than I'd like them to. I don't need to embarrass myself by mooning over her. But damn, her luscious ass feels good against my thighs. My cock starts to awaken.

Move faster, asshole. Don't press your inappropriate erection into her like a creep.

"Swing your arm back, nice and slow," I murmur near her ear.

She shivers. Because of me?

"Like this." I guide her arm and when she tries to fling the ball, I slow her down. It flies from her hand and—thankfully—doesn't roll into the gutter. Nor does it knock all of the pins down, but it hits a few and that's an improvement.

She spins around, beaming, her lips shockingly close to mine. "We did it!"

"You did it," I correct, entranced by those soft lips. I've yearned to know how they'd taste for years, and I'm not used to having them so close. If I move a few inches, I'll finally know.

But she's not mine, and if I know, I can't un-know. Better not to open that Pandora's box. With a burst of willpower I didn't know I had, I step away.

"Try again, all by yourself."

She nods, and grabs another ball. Biting her lip in concentration, she moves her body through the same motions I guided her through—or at least, her approximation of them. The ball sails along the lane and takes out another three pins. I clap. Devon cheers. Sydney throws her arms around me and somehow I manage not to hold her for longer than I ought to.

When I sit down, Sydney and Lena excuse themselves for a trip to the ladies' room, and Jase leans closer to me. "Bro, you've got to tell her how you feel."

"I can't," I mutter in response, irrationally afraid that she can somehow hear me. I've never mentioned my feelings to Jase, but it's clear he's read me better than I thought. I shouldn't be surprised. He comes across as a hotheaded jock but he's more attuned to emotions than he lets on.

Devon, on the other hand, furrows a brow. "Wait, what?"

"You can't tell?" Jase asks dryly. "Gabe has been mad about Sydney since before we met."

Devon's jaw drops and he blinks a few times, then closes it and swallows. "*Oh*." He nods to himself. "Yeah, that explains a few things." He gives me a searching look. "Dude, why haven't you done anything about it? Another guy could come along and snatch her up at any moment."

I glare at Jase, pissed that he'd out me like that. "She deserves someone who can give her more than I can."

Devon snorts. "More than a mansion, cool in-laws, and a heart full of love?"

Cringing, I lower my gaze to the floor. It sounds so cheesy when he phrases it that way. Why did Jase have to open his big fucking mouth? And why does he have to be so astute?

"Someone who can give her time and attention."

"If you haven't given it a chance, how do you know?" Devon challenges.

"I can't take a chance without risking our friendship, and I'm not willing to do that."

Jase tilts his head from one side to the other. "I can see both sides of this argument. But Gabe, are you really going to be able to watch her hook up with some other guy? Because I saw the way you were looking at her just now, and it's more than a crush. You were looking at her like I look at Lena."

I swallow, and I can't answer his question because I really don't know.

Either way, I'm fucked.

5

SYDNEY

"Coleman, can you check on the knee replacement patient?" Dr. Nazar, one of my supervisors, asks as he passes me in the corridor the following week.

"Yes, sir." I head for the room where the patient we operated on a couple of hours ago is recuperating. "Hi, Mr. Potts. How are you feeling?"

Edmond Potts, the middle-aged father of four teenage boys, smiles blearily up at me from the bed. Beside him, his wife is seated in a visitor's chair, holding his hand.

"Fine unless I move," he jokes.

"You've kept your sense of humor," I say. "That's a good sign." Sometimes that's the hardest part. People tend to think of surgery as an end game, but it's really only the beginning of the recovery journey. I check him over and am about to add my notes to his chart when Ken, another of the surgical residents, pokes his head around the door.

"Sydney, can I see you once you're done in there?"

Bemused, I nod. I don't know what Ken needs me

for, but he's a nice guy so I don't mind helping him out. I finish up and find him waiting in the hall. He's handsome in that prep school way some men have, with neat blond hair, expensive leather shoes, and teeth that have been whitened to within an inch of their life. He flashes them as I approach.

"What can I help you with?" I ask.

His smile becomes lopsided, almost playful. "It's something personal, actually."

My muscles stiffen. I'm not sure I like the sound of that, but I try to hide my reaction. "Oh, yeah?"

"Yeah." He shifts from one foot to the other, staring at me in an appreciative way he hasn't done before. "I saw your profile on Match-Me."

"Oh." Is he going to make fun of me for internet dating? Or does he think the fact that I'm on there means I'm up for a casual fuck? Because I'm not a casual kind of girl. Crossing my arms, I instinctively shield myself. "And?"

"And," he says with a grin, "I wondered if you'd like to go out to dinner with me."

"Excuse me?"

He shrugs. "I've been interested in you for a while, but I always got the vibe you were unavailable. Now I know you're on the market, I'd like a chance with you. That is, if the interest is mutual."

One part of what he said catches my attention. "What do you mean, I seemed unavailable?"

"Just that." He steps to the side as a gurney hurtles down the hall, and I follow. The result is that the two of us are now pressed against the wall, too close for comfort, and the conversation adopts a new level of intimacy. "I thought perhaps you were seeing someone. There was just something about you that didn't invite attention, and I thought you were trying to avoid it."

"Wow." I hardly know what to say. Have I really been giving that impression? Have I been so wrapped up in Gabe and our friendship that I shut myself off to anyone who might want to know me better, without even being aware of it? I suppose anything is possible.

"Well, I'm single. Have been for, oh, three years, give or take. The job doesn't exactly lend itself to dating."

He gives me a conspiratorial smile and a wink. "That's why I thought we'd be such a good idea. We see each other all day long."

I laugh. "So you want to take me out to dinner for the sake of convenience?"

His gaze wanders down my body again, and the smile fades. "Not just that. You must know you're beautiful, Sydney, and damn smart."

"Thank you." My cheeks heat, and I have no doubt I'm blushing, although thankfully it's difficult to tell with my skin tone. I'm not used to men being so forward with me. For the first time, I consider Ken as boyfriend material. He's cute, friendly, intelligent, and hardworking. Not to mention his future is secure—he's the best resident in the group, excluding me.

"So, is that a yes?"

"Yes." For the first time, I actually feel excited about the prospect of a date. Ken is someone I could really see a future with, assuming he wants the same things I do. I picture it. Sneaking kisses when we pass in the hall, eating together in the cafeteria, buying a little house with a front garden and cute retro wallpaper. A home. That's what I want. A place and a person with whom I can belong. That person could be Ken.

"Thank God." His expression is relieved. "I was worried I'd crash and burn. Where do you like to eat?"

"There's this Italian diner a few blocks away, Moretti's. Do you know it?" As soon as I mention it, I feel guilty. Moretti's is the place where Gabe and I go. I shouldn't have invited him there. But the damage is done, and I can't take it back.

"No, but I love Italian, and I'm sure I can find it," he says. "Are you free tonight, around eight?"

"How about seven?" I suggest. "I crash pretty quickly after my shift ends."

"Sure thing." His grin is so broad it could blind me. "I'll see you then, Sydney."

I return his smile. "I'm looking forward to it."

GABE

I haven't seen Sydney since bowling, although we've messaged a few times. On Friday, the night before my fight, I'm eager to see her in person. As soon as training ends, I head home and make myself presentable, then take my motorcycle to her apartment. I let myself into the building, but when I knock on her door, there's no response, and when I peek under it—yeah, I know that's a fucking creepy thing to do, but it's better than waltzing in unannounced—it's dark inside. She's either in bed, or out somewhere. Considering it's not yet eight, I'm willing to bet she isn't asleep. Of course, there's always the chance she had to work a long shift, but there's a crawling discomfort in the pit of my stomach telling me she's out somewhere with another man. I haven't heard anything about her dating plans this week, but considering she started off with a roar, I have no doubt she's still scoping out her options.

Or maybe she's not. Perhaps I'm getting all worked up about nothing.

I call Lena.

"Hi, Gabe," she says.

"Sydney isn't at her place. Is she there?"

She sighs. "Sorry, but no. I haven't seen her today."

Damn. "Any idea where she might be?"

"Gabe..."

My throat tightens, as does my grip on the phone. "Is she on a date?"

"I don't know." Lena exhales softly. "If I had to guess, then yeah, she probably is. I'm sorry."

I'm going to be sick. Apparently everyone is aware of my feelings now. Everyone except Sydney, who is off blissfully whiling away her evening with some guy who might decide he wants to call her his.

"Don't be sorry. She's allowed to see whomever the fuck she wants." Now I'm swearing at my brother's girl, because *that's* really going to go over well. "I gotta go, Lena."

Hanging up before I can make the situation worse— since I'm 100% certain she'll relay our conversation to Jase—I return to my bike, hop on, and consider my next step. I made the effort to clean up, so I don't want to slink back home. On impulse, I ride past Moretti's. As I pass, I see something that wrenches my heart from my chest. Sydney is at the window table with another man, and they're sharing a bowl of something, both of them smiling. I skid to a halt, ignoring the guy behind me, who shouts out the window and flips me the bird.

By now I've passed the diner, so I walk my bike to the side of the road and back up. As they come into

46

view, the guy reaches across the table and touches her hand.

I see red.

I want to wrench his arm from its socket and toss it in the nearest dumpster. What does he think he's doing, touching her like that? Doesn't he know she only likes to touch people she's comfortable with? But then she turns her hand over and clasps his. The action strikes me like a blow. Next thing I know, my helmet is slung over the handlebars and I'm striding inside. I made no conscious decision to move, and the horror on Sydney's face when she sees me is almost comical, but I'm committed now. There's no bowing out.

"Hey, Syd," I say, praying that steam isn't billowing from my ears. "I was driving past and saw you. Thought I'd stop and say hi. Who's your friend?" I emphasize the word "friend," eyeballing his hand where it's linked with hers. The guy is either brave or stupid because he doesn't move it, and while Sydney fidgets, she doesn't release him, either.

"Gabe." She straightens, drawing my attention to her top, which is loose and flowy and too low-cut. She wore it for him, and my hands itch to knock him out because of it. "This is Ken. We work together at the hospital. Ken, this is my friend Gabe."

"Nice to meet you." Ken disentangles his hand from Sydney's to shake mine.

"Yeah," I grunt. "Same here."

Despite my glare, he doesn't so much as cower. It seems like Sydney found a man who isn't scared of me. A doctor, no less. Way to make a guy feel inadequate. Especially when this particular doctor has the kind of face women gush over. I bet the ladies line up at his door. Plus that Ivy League education I can sense from a mile off means he's smart enough to go for Sydney.

At least I'm tougher than him. If this were centuries earlier, I'd have beat him to a pulp and claimed her as my prize. Unfortunately, that kind of attitude is exactly the sort of thing that would piss her off.

"Shouldn't you be at home, resting up and doing some last-minute research?" she asks, and it's blatantly obvious she wants me to leave. As for me, I want to hit something. Preferably Ken's face. But she's right, I have things I need to do.

"Will you be at my fight tomorrow?" I desperately want to know she'll be in the crowd. Sydney has always been my biggest cheerleader and seeing her as I walk to the cage gives me all the encouragement I need to win. Even when she looks terrified. Hell, *especially* when she looks terrified. In her eyes, I want to be the biggest, baddest dude out there.

"Yes, of course." Finally, she smiles. "I haven't missed one yet, have I?"

"Except for that time—"

"When Mickey Torres beat you," she finishes, rolling her eyes. "It was six years ago, and I know you have that weird superstition that you lost because I wasn't there, but he was more experienced, and that's all there is to it. If I'd been there, I would have seen my best friend get beaten, and then you'd have suffered a blow to your pride and I'd have been upset."

"It's not a weird superstition," I mutter. She's my good luck charm, and she knows it. But frankly, I'm annoyed she brought up my one loss in front of Dr. Ken. "I'll see you, then."

I nod and go, before I can do or say anything more I regret.

6

SYDNEY

Maybe I'm sadistic, but as much as I care about Gabe, seeing him so wound up over me being out with someone else is really gratifying. Maybe it's finally hitting home that I won't wait around for him forever. I have my own life to live.

Ken shakes his head. "That guy is intense. What's his deal?"

"He's an old friend of mine," I explain. "We grew up together."

"Your *best* friend, you said."

The way he says it, I can't tell whether it's going to be a problem. No matter how badly I want to find love, I won't be with someone who can't handle my relationship with Gabe, so I need to know if it's a deal-breaker.

"He's a professional MMA fighter," I say, as casually as I'd tell him that Gabe is a barista or an accountant. "In fact, he's fighting tomorrow night. Why don't you come with me?" If there's one surefire way to test his mettle, it's bringing him to watch my hot male best friend crush his opponent in the cage.

49

"Really?" His eyes light up. "That would be great. I don't keep up with the UFC, but I love live sporting events. The atmosphere is always incredible."

Okay, this guy is too good to be true. Not only is he willing to come despite Gabe giving him the scary glare, but he's actually excited for it. I should have hearts in my eyes, but all I can think is... he isn't Gabe. He's handsome, clever, and determined, but I don't ache for him to hold me, or yearn for his kiss. Maybe that will come with time.

Shortly after, our mains arrive. Ken eats carefully, dissecting everything he puts in his mouth. It's a strange sight because I'm used to the boys from the gym digging into meals with gusto. But I suppose Ken is like me, and doesn't often have time to exercise despite being on his feet all day. He needs to be more careful.

"Tell me what I don't know about you," I say after he declines the dessert menu—to my disappointment.

Steepling his fingers, he watches me over them. "I'm the oldest of three boys. Grew up in Chicago and moved here during high school after my mother and my stepfather met online."

"Quite a change from Chicago to Vegas."

He nods. "It was a big adjustment, but I love it here. Wouldn't be anywhere else. What about you?"

"I'm a local, born and bred."

"Do you have siblings?"

"No, it's just me." And thank God for that. I hate to think what would have happened if my parents had another child to ignore. They weren't neglectful, per se. I always had food and shelter, but affection was another thing entirely. To this day, I'm not sure whether they love me, or if they just had a child because it was the appropriate thing to do at that particular stage of their life. I like to think I made it through my childhood without being too screwed up—although I admit to craving physical contact and approval more than other people seem to.

"You must be close to your parents, then," he says, misreading me.

I laugh. "Quite the opposite. Actually, I used to pretend Gabe's mom was my own."

He doesn't appear to know how to take this, and I'm not sure why I shared it, even though it's true. The difference between my home and the Mendoza household, where his mother Valentina would bustle around in the kitchen while singing in Spanish, was stark. If I could have spent all of my time there, I would have.

"Anyway," I say, to cover the awkwardness. "Isn't it funny how we come from different backgrounds and still ended up in the same place? Life works in mysterious ways."

"That it does." He chinks his glass against mine, and we both drink. When he sets his glass down again, his expression is serious. "I have to ask, Sydney, why now? What made you decide to get back into the dating game?"

I sputter, choking on my drink. I wasn't expecting such a direct question. "Honestly, I'm sick of being alone, and I finally figured out that if I want someone to spend my life with, I need to go and find them." I hope I haven't put him off by being too serious too fast. But then, if he doesn't want a relationship, it's probably best I know now. I don't get that impression though. Something tells me he's in this for the long haul. "What about you? What are you looking for, Ken?"

"That's simple," he replies, still watching me steadily. "I'm looking for a life partner."

I stare at him, taken aback by his honesty.

"What?" The edges of his smile creep up. "Didn't expect me to be so upfront about it?" He leans forward, reaching for my hand, and I turn it over so his palm rests on mine. "I'm here at this diner with you because I think there's a real chance we could be a good match. Permanently. I need to know if you're on the same page as me, or there's no point in us seeing each other again. At least, not romantically."

"I'm totally on the same page as you," I say quickly. "That's what I want, too. But I've never thought about you this way before, so I need a little time to get used to the idea. I can't make a commitment to you right this minute."

He squeezes my hand. "I get that. But I'd really appreciate it if you could let me know whether you want to give this thing between us a real shot within a couple of weeks. Think on it." With that, he lifts my hand and kisses my knuckles. His lips are soft. They feel pleasant, but there aren't any tingles or flares of excitement.

"I can absolutely do that." I just need to get my head around this situation first. "And you should know how much I value you being open with me. Not many guys would be."

He shrugs. "Any man who doesn't make it clear where you stand isn't much of a man, in my opinion."

Jeez. Does he realize he just insulted Gabe? Probably. There's a smugness to his smirk that wasn't there before. Ken may be direct, but he isn't above taking potshots at others.

We finish the date and he walks me home. Outside my apartment building, he pauses and smiles down at me.

"I had a nice time tonight," he says.

"I did too," I agree. "Thanks for suggesting it."

"No problem. I'll see you tomorrow?"

I nod. "I'll text you the details. Goodnight."

"Goodnight." He doesn't move, and nor do I. Is it customary to kiss at this point in the evening? I'm so out of touch with dating that I have no freaking clue. Eventually, he ducks his head and brushes his lips over mine. The kiss is feather-soft, and once again, does nothing for me, thanks to Gabriel-freaking-Mendoza ruining me for other men. *Sigh*.

"Goodbye," I murmur, as he turns to leave. All the while, I'm wondering how I'm supposed to get out of the lust-web I'm caught up in when it comes to Gabe. It might take a while longer than I'd hoped.

GABE

"Get your head in the game," Seth growls as Jase pops me on the cheek.

I don't mind taking the hit, and ignore his rebuke. I've got this fight tonight, no problem. In truth, it's just a warmup for my match against Leo Delaney, AKA the finale of the Ruby Knuckles. Hell, I'm more nervous about seeing Sydney after today's event than I am about stepping into the cage. I do this shit all the time, and Taz Montgomery is a small fry compared to some of the guys I've been up against.

"Asshole, you hear me?" he demands.

"Yeah," I answer dutifully, but my mind is wandering to Sydney and what she'll be wearing. She always makes a big deal of these events and the atmosphere really gets to her. I hope that, however she chooses to dress, it's sexier than the outfit she wore for

Dr. Ken yesterday. Selfishly, I cross my fingers that she'll opt for the "Mind-Reader Mendoza" supporter gear— then everyone will see my face on her and stay the hell away. No one wants to mess with a fighter's girl. Especially not when that fighter is the son of a former champion and a wall of solid muscle.

"He knows what he's doing," Dad says from his seat against the wall. He tries to let Seth take charge at these events, and restrict himself to the role of manager, but it doesn't come easily to him. "It won't go for more than one round."

Seth's jaw tightens. "We'll see."

The medic checks on me, and then I'm escorted to the arena. The place has a high roof, bleachers around the walls, and rows of seats ringing the center stage. As usual, I called earlier in the day to reserve ringside seats for Sydney. As we make the journey to the cage, my eyes search the crowd for her. Finally, I find her, thanks to the bright overhead lights glinting off Lena's flaming red hair. But who's that on her other side?

I crane my neck. *Tell me it's not the bastard from Moretti's.*

It is. As I draw level with her, I can see him clearly. She brought a *date* to my fight? What the fuck is with that? This is *our* thing. Mine and hers. She doesn't get to invite every guy who wants to stick his dick in her— that's not how this works.

And what does it mean that she brought him here? If he warranted a second date, she must think he has potential. Surely she wouldn't let just any jackass come between us.

At the cage, the umpire checks that my mouthguard is in place and I stride to the corner, but my mind is whirling. I barely even see the guy opposite. I get an impression of purple silk and tattoos on white skin, but that's it. Glancing over at Sydney again, I try to see Dr. Ken's face. Is he smug? I bet he is. Why wouldn't he be? He's got the girl, and meanwhile I'm the one who has to go toe-to-toe with some fucker who thinks 'Taz' is a real name.

The umpire calls us to the center of the cage. He reels off the usual spiel, and we bump gloves. I'm expecting to win within one round, which is why it's a surprise when an uppercut appears out of nowhere, jarring me senseless. I stare at Taz, unable to believe he landed such a cheap shot. Where are my usual preternatural instincts? My ability to see a punch before it's even thrown? His fist comes at me again, and I slip out of the way, then counter with a kick across his gut. It knocks the air from him, but he smells blood and keeps on coming.

I feign a lunge, and when he tries to stop me with a push kick, I take his bottom leg out from under him. Seth screams at me to pin him down, but I'm too slow and he rolls upright, bouncing lightly on the balls of his feet.

Why is this guy still fighting? I should have dealt with him by now, and both me and the audience know it. Something is wrong. Embarrassed by my inaction, I take the initiative, striking at him with a combo I've practiced hundreds of times.

Wrong move.

I'm a counter-fighter, and leading the action isn't my style. Because of that, I'm unprepared when he ducks my punch, grabs me around the middle, and throws me to the ground. Unlike me, he moves fast, straddling my waist and rearing back for a knock-out hit. The beeper sounds, and the round ends. His expression betrays his disappointment. He climbs off me and returns to his corner. Hauling my heavy ass off the ground, I do the same.

"What the fuck are you doing?" Seth grabs me by the shoulders and shakes, as if Taz hasn't beat me up enough. "Head out of ass, Mendoza. Forget about whatever the hell your problem is—I promise, it'll keep—and focus on not dying."

7

SYDNEY

The instant the bell rings—only moments before Taz could deliver what was sure to be the final punch of the fight—I turn to Lena. "What the hell was that? What's he doing out there? He's letting that guy kick his ass!"

Oh my God, I'm going to kill him. If Taz Montgomery doesn't do it first.

"He's out of it," Lena says, trepidation in her eyes. "And he keeps glancing over here."

I'd noticed the same thing, and damned if it hasn't made me wonder whether this is some kind of sick payback for bringing Ken to his fight. As soon as the possibility enters my mind, I want to dismiss it, because surely Gabe isn't so messed up and masochistic that he'd take a pounding just to upset me, but I keep coming back around to it. The only other thing I can think of is that he feels so betrayed by my bringing Ken here that he can't focus—and surely that's too self-indulgent to be true. Why would he care that much

57

about me bringing a man along? It's ridiculous. He couldn't possibly.

And yet.

On the other side of me, Ken hums thoughtfully. "After how you sold him to me, I half-expected your friend to body slam the other guy and end it within thirty seconds. Maybe he's not as tough as you believe."

"Shut up," I snap, because his comment is not helping my peace of mind. "You don't know him like I do. He's got this."

"If you say so." He sounds dubious, and I don't blame him. Well... actually, I kind of do. If he's the reason Gabe is bleeding from a cut beneath his eye, I resent his presence, but I also resent Gabe's pigheadedness.

Lena thrusts something into my hand, and I glance down. A hip flask. Grateful, I tip it back, with no idea what's inside, and feel a burn down the back of my throat.

"Good, right?" she asks. "It's from Jase's liquor cabinet."

"Thanks." Wiping my mouth on my sleeve, I give all of my attention to Gabe in the cage, willing him to smash the other guy's face and be the fighter I know he is. My heart in my throat, I draw my knees up to my chest as the action restarts, grateful I'm not wearing a skirt. Whatever Seth said, it seems to have worked because Gabe doesn't falter once. It's clear to anyone who knows him that he's still shaken, but he's in control. His punches and kicks are snappy, and he takes his time gauging his opponent before making each move.

This is the version of Gabe I love to watch. Some people make the mistake of thinking he's passive because he waits for his opponent to screw up before attacking, but I think he's like a predator luring his prey into showing their belly. In this case, Taz lowers his guard for just a few seconds, and it's all over.

"Take him down!" I scream, as Gabe moves with far more grace than a man his size has any right to. "Go, Gabe, go!"

Gabe's foot whips into Taz's temple, and the guy drops like a rock. His eyes roll back in his head and he thumps to the ground. The umpire stands over him, counting. When he reaches six, Taz groans and tries to pick himself up, but then slumps into a heap. At eight, the umpire makes a slicing motion to indicate the fight is over. Gabe is victorious. The audience cheers, but he doesn't celebrate. He knows he screwed up tonight. Tension is visible in every line of his body, and in the stiff way he interacts with Seth, who hands him a water bottle. The announcer cries out that it's a win by way of knockout, and then the boys from Crown MMA, plus Gabe's dad, are heading out of the auditorium, passing us by, beelining for the back room.

I shoot to my feet. "Let's go, Lee." I turn to Ken. "Come on, we'll go say hi."

"Seriously?" He grins. "Awesome."

Together, the three of us make our way out. I flash my pass at the security guard, who admits us into the corridors behind the arena. When we reach the door marked "Gabe Mendoza," we pause outside. I can hear Seth ranting and don't want to interrupt his tirade. Awkward moments stretch out as we wait for them to finish, and finally the door swings open and Seth, Jase, and Devon stride out. I gesture for Ken to stay put, and slip inside to see Gabe. The medic is checking him over, but it's obvious the only thing injured is his pride. He looks sullen and angry—almost like a pouty toddler, except he's six foot three and solid muscle. Tomas Mendoza lingers in the corner and I wave at him. He smiles back, but it's strained.

"You're all clear," the medic says, as if it was ever in doubt. She smiles at me then leaves, closing the door quietly behind herself.

"You'll get him next time," Tomas says. "What you need to do is—"

"Later." Gabe holds up a hand. "Give me a moment with Sydney."

Tomas's eyes slide to me, and he hesitates but then nods. "You can't keep putting me off though, *mijo*."

He leaves, and when I hear the door click shut, I cross to Gabe and dab his bleeding cheek with my sleeve.

"You fought well," I say, and he just grunts. At this point in my life, I can interpret his grunts well enough to know he disagrees. "Okay, so maybe the first round was a loss, but you took him out pretty quickly after that."

I fuss with his cheek, where a bruise is forming, and he knocks my hand aside.

"I was distracted," he says, his tone accusatory. With my hands up, I back off. It's rare for his temper to show, but when it does, no one wants to be in his path. "I can't be expected to do my best when you're fucking with my head like this."

My lips fall apart, and a puff of outrage escapes. "Excuse me?"

He glowers, and it's obvious he didn't work out all of his issues in the cage. "What the fuck did you think would happen when you brought your new boyfriend along without giving me any warning?"

Wait a minute. Is he actually insinuating this is my fault?

What. An. *Asshole.*

In the face of his accusation, I throw caution to the wind and shove his chest as hard as I can. If it weren't for the shock factor, he wouldn't have budged at all.

"You know what, Gabe? Not everything is about you. Sometimes, things are allowed to be about me."

With that, I turn on my heel and storm out, only barely resisting the urge to slam the door behind me.

GABE

She's gone. Thank fucking God. I couldn't have handled her fussing over me for another minute without kissing her senseless and demanding to know what, exactly, she believes she can get from her date that she can't get from me. *Mierda.* I know I was an ass, but considering I just came close to losing to some no-name guy with a hick accent, I think I deserve to be ill-tempered for a couple hours. That asshole tasted victory—I saw it in his eyes—and Gabe Mendoza can't lose to someone like him. I can't.

Groaning, I wipe a hand down my face and consider what Dad will say when we talk later. He has high expectations, and while he didn't say it, I disappointed him tonight. He was so sure of me that he didn't even try to have a pep talk ahead of time, and then I nearly blew it. This will be great fodder for the sports tabloids. I've seen at least three headlines this year claiming I'll surpass Dad and win the Ruby Knuckles where he failed, but at least another four have declared that I'll forever be in his shadow. And now this. All of his hopes

—and years of supporting me—are hanging over my head.

Try living with that.

Someone knocks, and I ignore it. They'll go away. I need to be alone to stew in peace. But then the door cracks open.

"Hello?" It's a male voice. One I don't recognize. My stomach tightens with anger. Can't he tell he needs to leave?

"Fuck off."

"In a moment. First, there's something I need to say to you."

Opening my eyes, I scowl at Dr. Ken, who looks like he'd be right at home opposite Malibu Barbie. Except, in his twisted mind, Sydney is his Barbie. To his credit, Ken doesn't wither under the power of my glare as a lesser adversary might. That only pisses me off more. Why is he still here? Shouldn't he have left with Sydney? He won, after all. If he stays here, he risks me pounding him into the cement floor.

"The fuck you want?" I growl.

Ken approaches, arms crossed, expression smug. Of course it is. He has the girl. "I always wondered why Sydney didn't date," he says. "But now it's clear." He stops a few inches from me, and doesn't appear put off in the slightest by my bleeding face. "You've grown accustomed to having her attention, but that won't last now that she's finished waiting around for you. You didn't make a move, and she decided to put herself out there." Grinning, he cocks his head. "Thanks for messing up. You can be sure I won't make the same mistake. I fully intend to hold onto her, because I recognize something special when I have it, and I'll treat her as such." He shakes his head. "Seems like you set the bar low, bro."

My fists clench. I want to mop the floor with his perfectly symmetrical face, but then the truth sinks in. He's right. How many times have I stood Sydney up, or been late to a meeting with her? She's always smiled and waved it off, but I can tell it upsets her. I just haven't acknowledged what a dick I was being because she didn't call me on it, and no one else was around to see. But this guy—Ken—it's obvious he has his sights set on Sydney, and there's no reason for him to sugarcoat the facts.

I've been an ass.

Ken nods, even though I didn't speak my thoughts aloud. "Glad we've cleared that up. I hope we can get along better in future, now that we know where things stand. See you around, Gabe."

Then he leaves, taking my peace of mind with him. Swearing, I reach for the scissors and start cutting the tape from my hands. Now that I've opened a mental door, questions flood into my mind.

Have I taken Sydney for granted?

Do I expect her to support me and be in my life when I don't give her the same?

Yes, and yes. I'm a shit friend. Shame heats my cheeks and clogs my throat. When did our relationship become so one-sided? She's always been my safe harbor in a storm, and I'd thought I was the same for her, but a horrifying truth dawns: I'm not. I'm just another person who takes from her without giving back. Her date was right to call me on my bullshit.

"I'll be better," I whisper, but both Sydney and Ken are long gone.

Freeing my hands, I discard the wrapping and pace

over to the mirror. When I stare at my reflection, I don't like what I see. The man looking back at me isn't the man I want to believe I am. I've always relied on Sydney to be my conscience—the better part of me—but likewise, I've always believed I'd step aside when she found someone who could give her what she needs. Someone like Ken.

Yet now, every part of my body rebels at the thought.

Fuck that, Sydney is mine.

But if I want her, I need to work harder to deserve her, because right now, the guy looking at me in the mirror isn't good enough for Sydney Coleman, and he knows it.

8

_____

After kissing Ken goodbye outside my apartment building—a kiss that felt uninspiring and all kinds of wrong—I change into my pajamas. I'm quietly fuming about Gabe's behavior when a knock at the door catches my attention. Opening it, I expect to find that Ken has returned and already have a dismissal on my lips when I come to an abrupt halt.

Gabe stands there, dark eyes burning into mine, wearing a hoodie and track pants, and smelling of sweat and menthol. He shifts from one foot to the other, dropping his gaze from my face to the floor, looking less certain of himself than I've ever seen him. My heart—the stupid thing—aches to comfort him, but instead I take a step back.

"What do you want?" I ask.

"Is Ken still here?"

"No." He remembers Ken's name?

"Can I come in?"

If he showed any sign of the bluster from earlier, I'd refuse, but he doesn't. In fact, he seems to expect me to turn him away. Sighing, I step aside. Whatever this is about, it's clear there's something on his mind and there's no point in putting it off.

He enters, giving me a wide berth. "Thanks."

Since he's the one who came to me, I wait for him to speak first, not offering him an easy out the way I used to do. He hovers a few feet away, apparently struggling to find words. His internal conflict plays across his features, making him uncharacteristically easy to read. He's confused. Upset. But then his jaw firms in determination and with two strides he closes the gap between us and grabs me. His lips fuse to mine and his muscular arms haul my hips into alignment with his.

Uh, *what?*

My brain short-circuits.

After carefully keeping my distance from him for years because *hello*, he's my best friend, he obliterates it in one crushing kiss. Our lips rub over each other, and a shudder runs through me. The friction is exquisite, and he's literally stolen my breath.

Dear God, I might just die from sensation overload. It's so good. *Too* good.

I can't think.

This is a bad idea, but I can't remember why.

His lips ply mine open, and his tongue slips between, dragging a moan from deep within me. Desire flares, impossibly hot, as our tongues tangle. He tastes of spice and man—better than I ever imagined was possible—and I want to tumble to the floor and keep him there until I've satisfied my curiosity about whether every single part of him is just as delicious.

This is Gabe. Kissing me. *Why?*

I don't understand. I'm just a friend to him, aren't I? A pal, the same as Jase or Devon? But the way he's panting and gasping, his hands trembling as one curves around my breast and the other slides down over my ass, I get the impression that I've been wrong about everything. I'm not the only one who's fantasized about this moment. His big body vibrates with suppressed energy, and I want to know what it feels like when he unleashes it.

This is Gabe. Your best friend. Not some random guy. You need to stop. You need to be sensible.

But I don't want to be sensible. I want to know what it feels like to have the man I've adored forever make love to me. I press closer, desperate for more, and a low growl sounds in the back of his throat.

"Oh, my God," I breathe, astounded by how much the sound turns me on. But then, like a splash of cold water, I remember the man who just left. The one I was on a date with. Even if I crave Gabe with every fiber of my being, he can't give me what I need. What I *deserve*.

Gathering all my strength, I plant my palms on his chest and push.

"What the hell are you doing?" I demand, sucking in gulps of air.

He crowds me, clasping my upper arms in his giant hands and robbing me of my ability to think straight. Every brutal line of his face could be etched in marble. His expression is torment fueled by desire.

"I fucking hate seeing you with someone else," he snarls, his face only inches from mine, black eyes so intense that my heart flips and dances. He's towering over me, making me feel small and fragile, and I'm not sure whether I love it or hate it. "I know it's late in the game, but I want a chance with you."

"You—wait, what?" My mind cannot handle this. "What's going on here?"

The lines of his face ease as he brushes his lips over my forehead, so softly my knees quake in response. "I know we've always been friends, and lately I've been a shitty friend. For that, I'm sorry. But I want a chance to be more. Fuck, I want so much more with you. I have for years."

My lower lip wobbles. If this is a joke, it's a really mean one, because my stupid heart doesn't remember all the times he wasn't there, it only hears his declaration and thumps joyfully.

"Where is this coming from?" I ask, searching his unfathomable eyes for the answer. "If you're feeling threatened, you don't need to. I'll always be your friend. I'm sorry if I haven't shown that lately. I've been angry."

"Rightly so. I've acted like a jerk to you." He walks me backward until I feel the wall behind me. "But that's not what this is." Dipping his head close to mine, he nuzzles my neck, then inhales deeply. I melt, glad the wall is there for support because otherwise I'd be a puddle on the floor. Gabe is a passionate guy—not that most people would believe it—and when I'm the subject of his single-minded focus, it's potent and addictive. "I've wanted you ever since I walked in on you with that French guy in college." With this confession, he presses even closer, letting me feel the hard outline of his cock behind his sweatpants.

My eyes flutter shut. *Oh, sweet Jesus.* "Th-that was a long time ago."

"I know," he rumbles, running the tip of his nose along the curve of my throat. I tremble, hardly able to believe that he's touching me like this. Talking to me like this. It's all I've ever wanted, and yet I'm afraid to have faith in it.

"I'd never seen you naked before, but once I did, I

couldn't get you out of my mind. Those perfect tits, all soft and bouncing. That gorgeous round ass." He palms my butt and groans. "Fuck, it feels as good as it looks." His fingers sink deeper. "I've wanted to do this for so *damn* long." I open my mouth, but he silences me with a finger to my lips and raises his eyes to mine. "I'm not finished. You want to know what I remember most of all?"

I nod.

"I remember the look on your face. *Mm.*" He runs his hands up the side of my body, and every nerve fires. Heat pools low in my belly, and I'm so wet for him I'm a little embarrassed by it. Especially since the shock of his advance hasn't worn off yet. "I almost ripped that fucker off you. I wanted to be the only one who gave you that goddamned erotic, blissed-out expression."

He did?

"You never said."

"Of course I didn't." He scoffs. "We were friends. I didn't want to admit I'd started fantasizing about your mouth on me every time I jerked off. I might have scared you away, and I couldn't bear that. Then, later, I didn't think I could give you what you needed. But now, if you let me, I'm going to make certain I do."

Even as his words give my soul wings, my heart sinks. They're exactly the reminder I need that hot or not—and love him or not—Gabe is unreliable. He gives everything to his career, and has nothing left over for anything or anyone else.

"Why should I think things will be different?" I ask.

"Because I give you my word," he says, and I can tell he actually believes it. Whether he'll keep his promise once the luster wears off is another story. "I can see your doubt, and I'm not gonna lie, it hurts. But I can understand why you don't trust me. Keep in mind though, that if you say no and keep dating other people, this unresolved heat between us isn't going anywhere, and do you think that's fair for them?"

"No," I whisper, although I hate to admit it. "But what about our friendship?"

He closes his eyes. "I hate the thought of messing up what we've always had, but I'm pretty sure everything has changed whether we go any further or not."

He's right. I can't forget what it feels like to have his cock pressed against the V of my thighs, no matter how much I want to. The sensation is burned into my brain. But what if I give in to our attraction and make love with him, and he somehow works all of this pent-up desire out of his system? I don't know if I can handle his rejection once I know what it's like to truly be with him. My throat tightens as tears threaten. Why does this have to be so hard? Why do I have to yearn for him like this when I know it's bad for me? He's an addiction I can't shake.

"Baby, please. *Cariño.*"

My chin snaps up. He's never called me that before, but I like it. It feels right.

We feel right.

Calmness descends on my muddled mind. I've made my decision. I'm screwed anyway, so why not get an experience out of it that I can treasure?

Besides, I owe it to any future partner not to come to them with Gabe-related baggage. For that, I need closure.

GABE

If she doesn't give me this, I might spontaneously combust. I'm so turned on there's a legitimate possibility of my dick exploding, but I will not rush anything. Not when it comes to her.

Sydney, with her expressive brown eyes and flawless golden-brown skin. Sydney, whose soft tits are pressed into my upper abdomen.

I've given words to all of my messed-up cravings, put my heart on the line, and I can scarcely breathe as I wait to see what she'll decide. The cogs are turning in her mind. She's considering my request. Taking me seriously. I'm so close to having her.

So. Close.

"Did you and Ken discuss exclusivity?" I ask, desperate to dismiss the last of her concerns.

"No." The breath exits her lungs on a shaky exhale, tickling my neck. "It's only been two days. We're not together."

Thank fucking God. Despite hating him, I have a wary respect for the guy. He wasn't scared to put me in my place. If all I felt for Sydney was friendship. I'd probably approve of him. But I don't. Because Sydney is *mine*. Or she will be, as soon as I can talk her around.

"Tell me what I can do to convince you."

Her lips purse, and she draws in a slow breath. "I need to be treated properly. That means you make yourself available to do things with me that normal couples do. Like go on dates, or just hang out."

"Done." With my big fight only a short time away, I'll need to train for hours every day, but I'll make it work. I'll get up at four in the morning if that's what it takes. I can operate on very little sleep.

But her expression is skeptical. "I mean that, Gabe. I know you have a lot going on at the moment, but you

71

always do. That's just how things are with you, and if I settle for less than I want now in the hopes that things will improve, it will never happen. I know how you and Tomas operate. After the Ruby Knuckles, it'll be onto the next challenge. Let's do a trial run. If either of us decides it isn't working, you need to back off and stop sabotaging my dates."

My jaw clenches. "Agreed." I'll just have to make damn sure she has no cause to regret her decision. "But in exchange, you need to delete your dating app immediately. I'm not sharing you with anyone else."

She stiffens in my arms. "I'm not deleting it, but I promise not to use it until things between us are resolved one way or the other. Do you trust me?"

"I do." If either of us has proved themselves untrustworthy, it's me. Besides, I can hear in her voice that she thinks I'll mess up and give her reason to use the app again. But I won't. I *can't*. It's simply not an option. If I have to fit training in around time with her, then my dad and Seth will understand that, won't they? I swallow, my mouth dry. She's so fucking gorgeous, and finally, I'm on the verge of being able to touch her the way I've always longed to. Nothing else matters. I'll figure it out. "Are we really doing this?"

"Yeah." A smile curves her lips, and she caresses the side of my face. "I think we are."

"Good. Can we get to the kissing part now?"

She laughs, but the sound is nervous. I get it. We're taking a massive step. "Kiss me again, Gabe. And please, please don't stop."

That's all the permission I need. I tug her closer, rocking into the cradle of her pussy, as my mouth covers hers. She moans, and melts against my chest. She's boneless, and I support her with one arm while I learn the shape of her lips with my own. I've stared at them so many times. Dreamed of them. Imagined them around my dick while I got myself off, only to be riddled with shame afterward. But now, *finally*, I know how soft they are, and how sweet.

"Gabe." Her head flops back, and I graze my lips along the length of her throat, pausing on the delicate skin beneath her ear. She shivers. If I have my way, she's going to be shuddering a whole lot more than that. I intend to make sure she's completely satisfied by the time we're done, so there's no chance she'll even consider letting anyone else touch her ever again.

I nibble on her ear, taking my time, determined to draw this out and enjoy it, even if my erection is straining against my underwear and I'm legitimately concerned about coming in my pants before I get her to a bed. I'm not ashamed of it. I've wanted her for so fucking long that I'm certain if I do bust early, I'll be ready to go again within a few minutes.

"Did he kiss you like this?" I murmur against her throat, hating the possibility that I'm not the first guy to kiss her tonight. To touch her. I should have spoken up earlier, and owned my feelings like a man rather than behaving like a scared little boy.

"No," she gasps, clinging to my shoulders, her eyelashes casting shadows over her cheeks. "Not like this."

Satisfaction rips through me, overwhelming in its intensity. How did I ever believe I could let someone else have her? I *can't*. It's not in my genetic makeup. I need her more than air in my lungs.

"Good." My chest swells, and I have the insane urge to throw her over my shoulder, carry her to the bedroom, and lock her inside until she understands who she belongs to.

But then she guides my face up to hers and kisses me sweetly. Her tongue strokes mine, and I'm putty in her hands. Six feet three inches of pliable male. She kisses like she's craved me forever and has finally been allowed a sample. The perfect balance of shyness and confidence. She smells like the Sydney I know— coconut with a hint of disinfectant—and yet feels so different. I've never known the taste of her, or the sensation of her nipples brushing my chest, until now. Fuck, I want to see them. I can remember the color, clear as day. Dark plum, with areolas small enough for me to fit my mouth over.

Another wave of adrenaline crashes through me. I haven't come down from the rush of the fight yet, and when I try to ease my fingers beneath her waistband, they shake, making me clumsy. This is a recipe for disaster. Post-fight, I always need to fuck, but my hand is usually the only one who sees any action. I'm afraid of how carried away I might get with her. It's our first time, and I don't want to frighten her off just because I'm doped up on adrenaline and haven't been with a woman in more than a year.

"Baby," I pant, pulling back, my chest heaving. She looks up at me, her pupils swallowing the brown of her irises, making her eyes almost black. "I'm trying so hard not to overwhelm you, but I'm dying for you here, and if you want our first time to be gentle and slow, you'd better tell me to leave before we go any further. Because if you let me stay, I'm gonna fuck you over and over, and I can't promise I'll be completely in control of myself. So tell me if you can't handle that, 'cause in two minutes, I don't think I'll be able to make myself let you go."

Her expression softens. "I'm dying for you too, Gabe. I never imagined this would happen, and now it's like a switch has been flipped inside of me and I don't want it to end." She leans forward and brushes her lips over my cheek. "So don't you dare go anywhere, okay?"

"Okay." Her mouth hovers over mine, and we exchange breaths. In this moment, every part of me is alive and fully present. She centers me like nothing ever before. "I want to see everything you've kept hidden from me. Take off your clothes, *cariño*."

9
___

SYDNEY

Oh. My. God.

This is actually happening. Gabe is going to make love to me. I'm still struggling to accept the fact that the attraction between us is mutual. I mean, I've caught him checking me out a few times before, but the same goes for Jase and Devon, and I'm damn sure they wouldn't be reacting to me the way Gabe is now, like he's drowning and I'm his last breath of air.

This is all moving so fast my brain can hardly keep up, but perhaps that's for the best. I don't want to ruin this by overthinking it. I just want to feel all of the things I know Gabe is capable of making me feel. Taking his hand, I draw him into the bedroom. My apartment is small, because no single woman in her twenties with as many student loans as me could afford anything bigger, but despite that, I got a pretty great deal. I've often wondered if Gabe had something to do with that. He may not flash money around, but he has plenty of it.

The lamp is already on, casting an unexpectedly

romantic glow around the room, because I'd been in the process of preparing for bed when he knocked. His hands cup my shoulders as he comes up behind me.

His breath stirs the hair by my left ear, and then he whispers, "Let me see you."

I shiver, and his arms wrap around me, his fingers interlacing across my stomach. I tilt my head and he drops a soft kiss on the side of my neck, then nips the skin there with his teeth. Leaning into the shelter of his powerful body, I feel so safe and loved that tears spring to my eyes. Blinking them back, I tell myself not to be fanciful. He may care for me, but love has never entered the equation, and I'd be foolish to consider myself safe in the arms of the person who could hurt me the most.

Yet I do. And I want it to last forever.

Slowly, I pull away from him. Then I pivot and peel off my top, so all I'm wearing is pajama shorts, and panties. The panties are my favorites—vivid purple, which flatters my coloring, and I'm grateful for that as I shimmy out of them and the shorts in one movement.

"Oh, fuck," he mutters, his gaze locked on my body, skating up and down the length of me, not settling anywhere, as if he can't tell what part to pay attention to first. "Just look at you. You're the most beautiful thing I've ever seen."

My cheeks flame and I duck my head. No one has ever stared at me the way he is now. Blatantly and unapologetically. My skin tingles with awareness and my pussy is damp with arousal.

"I'm serious, Syd." He swallows, the cords of his throat moving. "You're fucking perfect. Better than I remember." He steps forward and raises a hand to trace the curve of my breast almost reverently. "I can touch you." He bends his dark head and draws the nipple into his mouth. I moan as his tongue flicks over the sensitive nub and he makes appreciative noises that are hotter than anything I've ever heard. He hums, the vibrations making me weak in the knees, and then releases my nipple with a wet pop. "I'm allowed to do whatever I want to you." Some kind of guttural growl bursts from him, and he settles his hands on my hips and drops to the floor. I realize his intention two seconds before he places his mouth over my pussy.

Pleasure bolts through me, and my back arches. "Oh, God."

His hands grip my thighs and he kisses me softly at first, teasing me with the tip of his tongue, sighing against me, but when I whimper, his gaze locks on mine and turns nearly black with passion. He gives one long, slow lick, then another. I gasp. His tongue moves against me as though he wants to know this secret part of me as well as he knows all the other parts. When I groan, he seems to lose control, and the gentle treatment ends. He devours me like a starving man at a buffet—lapping, sucking, and moaning, as if I'm the most delicious thing he's ever tasted. All of a sudden, I want the chance to do the same to him. To make him feel what I'm feeling now. But then his tongue burrows deeper and I lose the ability to think. He's merciless. My legs shake, and I clutch at his shoulders.

"I'm gonna fall," I gasp, and his hands grip onto my thighs more securely.

"I've got you," he promises, but he stands anyway and sweeps me off my feet, carrying me to the bed and placing me on it carefully, as if I'm fragile. My pussy throbs in the cool air, but he doesn't leave me waiting for long before he wedges his shoulders between my legs and slicks his tongue up my center.

"Mm." He nuzzles me, and I gasp. "Amazing."

"*Please*," I whimper as he teases me. "I need you."

He rises up, his eyes fastened on me, and wipes his mouth on the back of his hand. My lips part. He looks like he wants to do dirty, filthy things to me, and I've never wanted anything more.

"You sure?" He gives me one last out. As if I want one. All I want is him.

"Yes. A thousand times, yes."

"Thank God." His gaze heats and he straightens, the motion strangely graceful for such a big guy. It's only now that I notice he's still fully clothed, his dick pitching a massive tent in his sweatpants. "I need you, too, gorgeous."

His voice is tight with desperation and it makes me dizzy with power. Slowly, I slide my hands up my body, over my stomach, and around my breasts. Pressing them together, I squeeze and massage and flick the pads of my fingers over my dusky nipples, pretending they're his. The way his erection leaps behind the fabric of his sweats makes it all worthwhile.

"Your turn to get naked," I whisper.

Holding eye contact as much as possible, he strips off in ten seconds flat, and then he's bared for me in all his spectacular muscled glory. Rising up on my elbows, I admire him. Hulking shoulders, brawny chest dusted with hair, meaty thighs that make my mouth water, and the ink that dances across the top of his feet and up his calves. Then, finally, my eyes are drawn to his pelvis, where a swarthy cock juts proudly toward me.

I swallow. He may have seen me naked before, but this is the first time I've seen beneath his underwear, or truly allowed myself to look my fill. Until now, it's been stolen glances when I think he isn't looking, or ogling photographs of him from the safety of my bedroom. In the flesh, he's so much more than a good-looking man. He's full of vital energy and barely suppressed sexuality. I ache to have him inside of me.

"Come here," I say.

He approaches, his dick thick and heavy. I run my fingertips along the length of it and feel how hot it is. His muscles bunch and a long exhalation shudders through him. Precum beads at the tip and I lean forward and lick it off. His hips jerk.

"Fuck, baby. I can't..." He visibly strains to get a hold of himself. "Can't take much of that. I've practically been a monk, and you're all my fantasies come to life."

Satisfaction swells within me, both that I can have such a potent effect on him, and that he hasn't been sleeping with any of the fight bunnies who frequently come onto him.

"I want to drive you wild with my mouth," I admit. "I love the taste of you."

"Holy fuck." He gulps. "Later, I swear. Right now, I need your beautiful pussy." His hand dips between us and rubs my swollen clit. "You're so wet." His fingers slip between my folds. "I always knew you'd be like this."

My hips shift restlessly. I have an empty feeling that only he can fix.

"Fill me," I say, not taking my eyes off him. I don't have to ask twice. He grabs a condom from his wallet, tears it open, and slides it on without any finesse.

"So long," he murmurs, positioning himself atop me and notching into my entrance. "I've wanted this for so fucking long." Then, in one smooth motion, he thrusts home.

"Gabe," I gasp, and above me, he grits his teeth, air hissing between them. My vision blurs, and I'm so full of him. He's the perfect size to occupy those vacant spaces inside me. He's not even moving, and I'm poised on a precipice. "You feel amazing."

"God, Sydney. This must be what heaven is like."

Finally, he moves, and it's exquisite. My teeth scrape over my lower lip. At first, it's the slowest of thrusts, and he kisses me so tenderly I almost can't believe this is the same man who was engaged in a fist fight barely an hour ago. I push back against him, burying him fully within me, pleased when his breath hitches in a way that lets me know he's on the edge of his control. Grabbing his ass, I pull him deeper inside me than he's ever been, and he plunges over the cliff of reason into the same whirlpool of crazy desire that I've been fighting since he first kissed me. Grabbing my calves, he levers my legs up into the air and slams into me. Stars explode behind my eyelids. He repeats the movement, and it's all I can do to cling to him and experience the overload of sensation as he slides in and out. Deeper, harder, until he somehow becomes a part of me.

We've always been close, but never like this. Our souls fuse together as we breathe as one, move as one, and moan as one. He and I are intertwined in a way I've never been with anyone else, and it's so beautiful it brings tears to my eyes.

"You okay, baby?" he asks, spotting the wetness on my lashes.

"Perfect." I capture his lips. "Never better."

He smiles, his expression startlingly tender. "Me neither."

Angling his pelvis, he slides in deeper, his gaze holding mine. I whimper, and my eyes try to close, but I fight to keep them open. He does it again, hitting my clit just right, and between the fullness and the magic of my connection with him, it's too much. I break into a thousand glittering pieces, sobbing his name.

"*Fuck,*" he grunts. "*Sydney.*"

And then he's shaking above me, unloading everything he has into me, and his eyes are locked on mine the entire time. It's earth-shattering. There's no other word for it.

I'm never going to be the same.

He rests his forehead on the bed, then turns to drop a kiss on the side of my neck. Meanwhile, I stare at the ceiling, my heart thudding as fast as if I'd just received a new emergency patient at the tail end of a long shift. Slowly, he raises himself on his elbows and brushes my hair back with one hand.

"That was only the beginning."

I smile. "It had better be."

"I promise, *mi cariño.*" He rolls off me and swings his feet to the floor.

"What are you doing?" I ask, hating the uncertainty in my voice.

"Condom," he replies, peeling it off. "And I'll get something to clean you up."

"Oh, okay."

A moment later, he's back with a warm cloth, which he uses to clean me with gentle motions. When he's done, he sets it aside and touches two fingers to my chin, meeting my eyes with his unfathomable ones.

"Baby, I'm not going anywhere tonight. I'm all yours."

As I creep from the room, Gabe snores, and I jerk around, making sure he hasn't woken up. He rolls onto his back, an arm flung across his face, then doesn't move. Exhaling with relief, I take the opportunity to study him. Gabriel Mendoza is a stunning man, although many think him a brute. He's big, several weight grades above his training buddies, but none of that weight is fat. He's all muscle. Solid, rough-hewn muscle.

I lick my lips. Yum.

In his current position, his chest and abdomen are exposed, the blankets wrapped around his hips and lower half. His shoulders and arms, which held me all night, are relaxed, but still bulky. I name the muscles in my head. *Trapezius, deltoids, pectoralis major, latissimus dorsi, biceps brachii, triceps brachii, brachioradialis.* As far as the human musculoskeletal system goes, he's a spectacular example. He moves, turning onto his side, and everything ripples. I drool just a little, then I gather my scattered wits from the floor and head out to the living room, closing the door behind me.

In the wake of this momentous event—sleeping with Gabe after being his best friend since we were tiny —I need to sort out the mess of my romantic life, and that means clearing the field of any players except him, at least for now. I'm still afraid to trust that he'll dedicate himself to this relationship the way he said he would, but if it fails, it won't be because of anything I've done. Finding my phone, which I didn't want near me last night in case someone interrupted us, I select Ken's contact details and hit call.

"Hey, Sydney," he replies, sounding perky and awake. Perhaps he has a shift soon. "It hasn't even been twelve hours. This either bodes really well or completely terribly."

Guilt pierces me, but I do my best to ignore it.

"I'm afraid it's the latter. Gabe came by last night and made a tangle of everything. It seems like there are some unresolved feelings between us, and I really need to work them out before I decide whether to move on with another man. I'm sorry for leading you on, but I truly thought nothing would ever come of my soft spot for him."

Ken sighs. "I can't say this is unexpected. It only took me ten seconds to see he's crazy about you. That's why he came into the diner the other night, to stake his claim."

This conversation isn't making me feel any better, but then, Ken has every right to be annoyed with me. Mostly, he seems resigned. It could be worse.

"Again, I'm sorry. I wish I'd handled this without dragging you into it."

"It's okay," he says, proving what a nice guy he is. "You need to figure this out for yourself, and if you decide you don't want him, then call me. I'm not going to say I'll be waiting, because I don't know how long this will take, but I'd be interested in seeing you again if we both happen to be unattached at the same time in the future."

The corners of my mouth lift. "I'll keep that in mind. Thanks for being so understanding."

"No problem. Take care."

I end the call, feeling like a storm cloud has finally passed, and blue skies are ahead. How long will they stay that way?

10

_____

GABE

The first thing I become aware of is the ache in my face. The second is the smell. Sweet, feminine, very definitely not the odor of my bachelor pad. Then the memory hits me.

Sydney.

Kissing her, touching her, making her mine. But she isn't in bed with me. Why not?

Rising, I test my sore limbs. My legs are okay, considering I got knocked around more than expected. I transfer my weight onto them and venture out of the bedroom in search of my girl. I find her in the kitchen, pouring a mug of coffee, and one of herbal tea.

My heart flutters.

It goddamn *flutters*.

And all because I spent the night pleasuring a woman who knows me well enough not to give me caffeine. I don't drink the stuff. It messes with my energy levels, and I don't stand for anything doing that.

"Morning, beautiful," I say, coming up behind her

and dropping a kiss on her bare shoulder. Her hair is wild, with dark curls corkscrewing all over the place, and I know from experience that she'll freak out as soon as she notices. Me, though? I think it's gorgeous. She's never believed me when I tell her so.

"Hey, there," she replies, turning to kiss me. The faint brush of her lips isn't enough, and I pull her back for a second kiss, deeper and firmer. When I let her go, her cheeks are flushed and she's breathing heavily.

"That's a real kiss."

She rolls her eyes, but I know it rocked her as much as it did me.

"What do you want to do today?" I ask, taking the herbal tea and blowing across the surface.

She shrugs. "I'll probably do some stuff around the apartment. Lena and I talked about meeting up later."

Shifting from one foot to the other, I wonder whether I should read anything into the fact that her plans don't include me.

"I hoped you might come to the pool with me," I say. "I usually go the day after a fight to loosen up." Since her brows have drawn together, I add, "I'll swim a few lengths and then sit in the spa for a while. You could just head straight for the spa."

"Isn't your pool time when you finally get to be alone and decompress?"

She's got me there. But today, I don't want to be without her.

"I haven't seen much of you lately, and I want to spend today together."

She brightens until she's absolutely glowing. "All right then. I'd love to come with you. Do you want to eat first? I have smoothie ingredients."

"Nah, you have one. If I do, it'll give me cramps when I'm swimming. I'll eat after." An idea occurs to me. "We should go out for lunch." She wants to do things normal couples do, and what could be more normal than a lunch date?

Impossibly, her smile widens. "Count me in."

I touch my lips to her forehead, because I can't *not*, and take my mug to the nearest chair, where I watch while she prepares a smoothie. There's something so domestic about seeing her add bananas, oats, and vegetables to the blender after holding her all night long. My soul feels light. Like everything is at peace in the world, and nothing matters beyond this moment. She switches the blender on, and while it's whizzing, she comes over and straddles my lap. Cautiously, so as not to spill my drink, I kiss her. She loops her arms around my neck and snuggles in.

Damn, if every morning was like this, I'd never want to leave home. I'd quit the gym and stay with her forever. But she gets up, ending the moment, and goes to the blender to turn it off, then pours her smoothie into a tall glass. It's a gross color, somewhere between green and brown, but probably tastes better than mine do. I find it best to hold my breath while I chug my smoothies, so I don't taste them any more than necessary. In contrast, Sydney sips hers.

"That black eye looks like it hurts," she remarks.

"It's fine. Barely even notice it," I lie. "I let him get a couple of cheap shots in to build up his confidence before I took him down."

"Mmhmm." She smirks. "Of course you did."

She wants me to admit I saw her with Dr. Ken and freaked out, but it's not going to happen. I have some pride left, even after getting the stuffing knocked out of me by a no-name.

Once she's finished with her smoothie, we ride my motorcycle back to my place, then get an Uber to the pool—not the nearest one, which is cheap and crappy, but the great aquatic center I prefer to use. It comes with all the best conveniences. Spa, lane pool, sauna, and a load of gear anyone can hire. I have a VIP pass, which means I can come and go as I please, but we pause at the counter to pay for Sydney's entry. Bumping her aside, I cover the cost. It may be small, but I like to think it's a step in the right direction—something a man would do for his woman.

We go our separate ways to the changing rooms, and meet at the spa. When I see Sydney, my eyes nearly bug out of my head. She's wearing a yellow bikini that ties at the hips and the nape of her neck, displaying her mouthwatering body for anyone who cares to look.

And the men look.

As she walks, their eyes track her, and when she reaches me, I catch one asshole's gaze and stare at him until he turns away.

"Gabe?" she asks questioningly.

I grunt. "Let's get in the water."

We climb into the spa, and it's amazing on my aching body. I slide onto one of the benches along the edge and lift her onto my lap, so her ass is nestled over my dick. I don't care if it's too much PDA, all of these people need to know that this incredible woman is with me. Not to mention that it feels like days have passed since I last had her, rather than hours.

"I love this bikini." I rest one of my hands on her hip and the other on her thigh to hold her in place. "I haven't seen it before." If I had, I'd have lost my shit.

Heads would've rolled. Any guy who looked at her sideways would have known my wrath. And considering we were "just friends," that would've been awkward as hell to explain.

"We haven't been to the pool together in years," she says.

"That can't be right." I think back, but I don't recall any instance of us doing this since she left medical school and I went pro in the MMA circuit. Maybe we instinctively knew there were some lines we shouldn't cross. Some things friends aren't meant to see. "Well, I was missing out."

She leans back, resting her weight on my chest so I can see her face, and smiles mischievously. "Yes, you were."

We soak for a while longer, and as we do, we talk, catching up on all the parts of each other's lives we've gotten behind on recently.

"Does this feel weird to you?" I ask after a while. "You and me, together."

She studies me carefully, like she's wary of where I'm going with the question. "Actually, no. It feels natural."

I smile, and kiss her. "I thought so too. I expected it to be more of an adjustment, but being with you, I feel more myself than I have in ages."

Her eyes fill with tenderness. "Good.

We kiss again. Then, determined not to be one of those people who make others uncomfortable with their public exploits, I leave Sydney in the spa and swim a few dozen lengths of the pool. By the time I return, I'm far more in control of my hormones. At least, I am until I see that the vultures have descended. Sydney has been joined by a bulky black guy with broad shoulders that

89

suggest he spends a lot of time swimming. He's wearing speedos that are practically indecent, and leaning far too close to her for my comfort.

"Who are you?" I bark as I rest a possessive hand on her shoulder.

The guy raises a brow. He's tall and muscular—much the same size as me, which is fairly unusual—and clearly isn't used to anyone questioning him.

"Dean," he says. "And if you don't mind, I'm having a conversation with Sydney."

"Your conversation is over. Sydney's leaving now."

He glances at her, as if to check whether she needs help. Like I'm a crazy stalker or some shit.

"It was nice to meet you, Dean," she says, completely unaffected by my rudeness. "This is my boyfriend, Gabe. The one I was telling you about."

Satisfaction rips through me. That's my girl.

"Ah." His expression tells me he thought she'd been lying to put him off. Then he gives me a second look. "Gabe Mendoza? Fuckin' hell, I'm sorry, man. Didn't realize she was spoken for."

Narrowing my eyes, I give him my meanest glare. Sometimes there are benefits to being a public figure. "Yeah, well, she is. Come on, baby. Let's get out of here."

Sydney stands and takes the stairs out of the spa. When jerkface's eyes drop to her ass, I give him a pointed look. He shrinks back against the wall.

Yeah, that's what I thought. Coward.

"I told him I was here with someone," Sydney says as she wraps a towel around herself and pads toward the exit.

"I know you did. Some guys are crap at listening. Hey, come on." I grab her hand and lead her to the counter, where the woman behind the desk glances up expectantly.

"Can I help you?" she asks.

"We'd like to rent one of the private spas," I say, resting my hand on the small of Sydney's back so no one else can mistake her for being available.

The woman nods. "For how long?"

I check with Sydney. "Is half an hour enough for you?"

She smiles. "Sounds perfect."

"Great." I pay, and we follow the woman's directions down a long hall to our own personal spa room, which has an opaque glass door for privacy. Sliding the key into the lock, I open it, and steam billows out. I wait for Sydney to enter, then lock it behind us. "Now it's just you and me, baby."

I back her into the wall and kiss her, grateful to have her to myself again. A gasp escapes her, and I swallow it, grinding into her, wanting her to know that even though we've been fucking nonstop since last night, I want her more than ever.

"Whoa," she pants. "Slow down. We should make use of the spa, since you paid for it."

"What spa?" I ask. "Who cares about the spa?"

She laughs, and it fills the room like the sound of angels singing—or is that just in my head? "We have plenty of time later for *that*. This isn't the place."

"Fine." Grumbling, I put her down. "But just know that seeing you in that bikini drives me insane." We both sink into the warm water and face each other. Pressing my forehead to hers, I hold her smoky gaze and share her breath. My arms encircle her, and we float in a bubble of our own making. "Is this crazy?"

She exhales and her breath tickles my lips. "Maybe, but it might have been inevitable, too."

I close my eyes, feeling closer to her in this moment than I ever have to anyone else ever. "I think it's a good crazy. Tell me I'm not wrong."

Her mouth brushes mine. "You're not wrong."

11

_____

SYDNEY

Best. Day. Ever.

Morning sex. Spa pool. Making out with the guy I've lusted after forever. And now, lunch at a fancy restaurant that neither of us have been to before. Gabe Mendoza knows how to make a girl feel special, I'll give him that.

Yeah, he also knows how to make you feel unimportant and forgotten.

I push the comment to the back of my mind, but don't shut it out completely. It's a fact that I need to remember moving forward. Today isn't business as usual for Gabe. It's his quiet time to recuperate. In another day or two, he'll be back at the gym, unable to spend as much time with me as he is now. That's not necessarily a bad thing, or something I intend to hold against him, but I need to be cautious and not expect too much in case he crushes me—accidentally, of course. He'd never intentionally hurt me.

Even though I know that, I also know he wants to win the Ruby Knuckles almost as much as Tomas wants him to. He idolized his dad when we were kids, and loved being part of the gym's family—he could throw a punch before he could swim. And ever since Tomas's career ended with a devastating kick to the head, he's focused all of his attention on grooming his son to succeed him. As for Gabe? There's nothing he wants more than to make Tomas proud.

Opposite me, he sinks into an elegant wooden chair, looking stiff and slightly out of place. The restaurant—an upscale French spot—is not his usual scene, and I appreciate that he's willing to branch out for me, and push beyond his comfort zone.

"Wine, sir?" the waiter asks, addressing the question to Gabe.

"Not for me," he replies. "Syd?"

"Yes, please. The house white." I'm making the most of this date, day-drinking and all.

"No problem. I'll be back to take your order shortly."

"So, how's work lately?" Gabe asks when the waiter has left.

"Much the same as usual. The ER rotation is fast-paced and a bit difficult on the emotional front, but I'm picking things up quickly."

"I bet you are." He smiles. "You always work so hard, and it pays off. You're a perfectionist."

"Yeah, well." I touch my hair, making sure it's still confined within a bun. I can feel the fuzzy ends starting to stick out, but it's not too bad yet. "Takes one to know one."

He nods. "People expect a lot from me. Especially Dad. I can't let him down."

"But what about what *you* want?" I ask, echoing a common refrain in our conversations. While I approve of his work ethic and love of family, I've always questioned the way he accepts his dad's plans for his career without ever stopping to consider what he truly wants from life.

He shrugs. "I want to win the Ruby Knuckles." His expression softens as he watches me, and then he reaches across and takes my hand. "And I want you."

Freaking hell. The guy is a master of turning the tables, and man is he smooth. Even though I know he's trying to divert me, I can't help going gooey inside as he turns my palm over and kisses it. I close my eyes, battling the urge to shove the table aside and have my way with him right here, right now. I deserve a medal for resisting him as long as I did. Now that I know how it feels to have him inside me, I can't fathom how I ever thought I could keep him at arm's length. It was only a matter of time before we ended up here.

"What do you want, Syd?" he asks.

I want to be seen. I want to be loved. I want to be wanted.

But I'm a self-respecting woman, so I don't say any of that out loud. Instead I say the closest thing I can without tearing up. "I want to not be lonely anymore."

"Aw, baby." He kisses my hand again, then presses it to his cheek, his gaze locked on mine. "You won't be, *cariño*. I promise."

His intensity makes me shiver. I wish I could believe him. I want to, wholeheartedly, but this is Gabe, and I know him better than anyone. He's the king of overcommitting himself. So I suppose I'll just have to wait and see how this plays out.

After lunch, we go to the movies to watch a romantic comedy—Gabe's choice. Apparently he wants to cram the full dating experience into one day, and that includes sacrificing his manliness to watch something

95

I'll like. Twenty minutes into the film, his hand creeps over my thigh in the dark theater, then edges up and dips beneath the waistband of my pants.

"Behave yourself," I mutter, bur don't stop him as his hand travels deeper, settling over my pussy, which is already wet and throbbing for his attention.

"Stop?" he asks, his lips beside my ear.

"Yes." I don't want him to, but we have to draw a line somewhere. Unfortunately, as soon as he removes his hand, I rock toward it, seeking him out. It's a natural instinct, one I didn't expect, and I feel his lips curve.

"Liar," he breathes, his hand hovering above me, only an inch from where I want it most. I whimper. Why is he tormenting me like this? Why can't he just touch me? "Do you want it, baby? Or not?"

Furtively, I glance around. There's no one in our row, but the girls below us have given me the stink eye a couple of times.

His lips tease the edge of my ear. "Yes or no? 'Cause I'm having trouble keeping my hands off you."

I release a shaky breath, giving in to my what my body craves. "Yes."

"That's my girl."

He eases his fingers through my slick folds, and after the anticipation that's been building with every second he held off, my hips buck and my head drops back. He pushes one finger into me, cupping me with his palm, putting delicious pressure on my clit.

"Oh, God," I whisper.

"Shh." His soothing tone at odds with the commanding, masterful way he crooks his finger inside me. Holy shit, my hips rise even further, and I have to clench my teeth together to bite back a moan. I can't believe we're doing this. His fingers are inside me, and

96

meanwhile the film is still playing, and the other twenty or so patrons in the theater are none the wiser. Somehow, that only makes me wetter.

He moves his finger again, like he's summoning the wicked part of me out to play. Reaching over, I try to grab his cock so he knows the intense mixture of pleasure and frustration I'm experiencing, but he gently shifts my hand away, denying me. Then he leans closer and his mouth brushes my temple.

"You're like an addiction." His breath tickles my ear. "I've denied myself for so long and now that I've taken one hit, I can't get enough."

His words stoke a fire inside me because he's given voice to my deepest, most secret desire. I *want* to be someone's everything. To know that they can't function without me. I yearn for it. And perhaps a psychologist would say that's a result of growing up without much affection, but I think a lot of people feel this way, deep down. We like to be wanted, but we *love* to be needed.

"You'll never be lonely again," he goes on, pumping his thick finger deliciously. "Because every time you turn, I'll be there."

His palm squeezes around my pussy, and suddenly I'm on the edge. My breathing is shallow, and I'm on the verge of screaming his name and begging him to make me come. Turning in his seat, he covers my mouth with his, hushing any involuntary sounds that might escape. He works me with his fingers and I plummet into a spectacular orgasm, shivering and clenching around him. When I finally still, he extracts himself from my pants and sucks his fingers clean.

"I need you," he murmurs, voice rough. "I need to remind myself this is real. That I've had you, and I can have you again."

I snatch his magical hand and stumble to my feet. "Let's get out of here."

GABE

"Bro, how are you doing?" Devon calls across the room when I arrive at the gym on Monday morning. "Still pissed about the fight? Want to work out your anger on me? I'm up for some tough sparring."

I pretend not to hear him. If I give him nothing, perhaps he'll leave me be. I'm not sure how to break the news about me and Sydney, or whether I even should yet.

"Dev, you know his mood has shit-all to do with the fight," Jase adds, loudly enough that it's impossible to ignore him. "He's sour because Sydney's dating. That's what threw him off on Saturday. So," he strides over and bumps my fist, "did she tear you a new one when you went to apologize? Do I need to send Lena to do damage control?"

"Syd and I are fine," I say, and can't help but think of how *very* fine she is.

"Fuck off." Jase's jaw drops. "Did you finally make a move on her?"

Devon hoots. "He did! I can see it in his face."

When did I become so easy to read?

"Screw you, assholes," I say, in lieu of an answer. What's between Sydney and me is just that: between us.

Clapping me on the shoulder, Devon says, "Good for you. Took you long enough."

I force myself to laugh. "Yeah, well, good things take time, and they're usually worth the wait."

Jase crosses his arms and lifts his chin, giving me what —if I didn't know better—I'd call a Big Brother Stare-Down. "I'm happy for you, man. But if you hurt her, you'll be in a world of pain because we all care about Sydney. She's a great person. And, you know," he shrugs, "she and Lena are tight, which means I'm responsible for her virtue or some crap like that because no one else has ever done that for her." His eyes flick up and down. "Except you."

I've got to say, it's weird as fuck getting the hard word put on me by the guy I think of as a brother, but I'm glad he has Sydney's back. She deserves to have people looking out for her.

"I'll do my best. I want her happy."

He nods. "I know you do."

"Good. Can we be done with this conversation now?"

He tosses me a skipping rope. "Seth says thirty minutes, then we'll do power rounds. He'll partner with you."

Devon smirks. "You screwed up, man, and he's going to let you know it."

I was expecting this, but still, my heart sinks. Seth is like an older brother to all of us, and when he's disappointed, it's the worst. I look around. "Where is he now?"

"On the phone with his sister," Jase answers.

Devon's eyebrows shoot up. "He has a sister?"

"Yeah, they don't talk much." Harley Isles is a kickass fighter and has lived in Thailand for the past eight years. She's an absolute savage and does the family name proud. I have a feeling she and Seth have some kind of plan in the works, what with how much he seems to be talking to her recently, but that's just my personal hunch, and until I hear anything from him, I'm keeping it to myself.

I start skipping, and after that, training passes quickly. My body is sore from the fight, but not so sore that anyone needs to baby me. Strangely, despite how much I enjoy locking myself away at the gym, today I'm eager to leave. It feels like days since I've seen Sydney, and I'm excited to kiss her and reassure myself this hasn't all been a dream. The boys and I eat lunch together, and then return for another training session, this time working on our technique with pads and partner drills. We finish with an hour of jiu jitsu, and I shower and change as quickly as I can, but when I get the chance to call Sydney, I see she's already messaged.

Sydney: *Working a double shift. Can't see you tonight. Hope training went well. XX*

Disappointment floods me, and all the hype that I've built over the day crumbles. Man, this sucks. I've been getting myself through endless rounds of punches and push-ups by picturing her face and all the dirty things I intend to do to her once we're alone. And now, nada. No bedroom antics for Sydney and me. At least she messaged. Imagine my disappointment if I'd gotten all of the way to her apartment only to find it empty.

A lead weight drops in my gut. Jesus, is this how she feels when I bail on her because of training, or when I'm so late she's practically napping on her dinner plate by the time I get there?

If so, I'm a shitty person. But I'll be better. For her, I have to be.

12

GABE

Since I've got no hope of seeing Sydney, I head to Mama and Dad's place instead. They own a white stone house not far from mine, and I knock on the door a little while after dinner time.

"Gabriel!" Mama beams up at me, her deep brown eyes crinkling at the corners. Even though she's fifty this year, her crow's feet are just beginning to form and only a few strands of gray have dared to show themselves amongst her mane of dark hair. She wraps me in a hug. She smells of paprika—no doubt from dinner—and lemon, from the soap she favors. "*Hola.* It's so good to see you!" She squeezes me tighter as if it's been months since I visited rather than a week or so. She stands back, holding onto my shoulders, studying my face. "You look good, *mijo.* You should have come earlier. I would have fed you."

"I didn't want to mess with your dinner plans."

"Oh, please." She swats my shoulder with one delicate hand. Another thing about my mama? She's a good foot shorter than me. "You could never." She steps aside to let me in. "There are leftovers if you want some."

"No thanks, *Mama.* I've eaten."

She sighs. "Why don't you let me look after you anymore?"

I drop a kiss on her cheek. "Because I'm a grown man. I look after myself."

She shakes her head wistfully. "Mothers should always look after their sons."

"Is *Papa* here?" I ask, not having seen him.

"In the living room." She waves a hand in that direction. "Watching the fight from this weekend." Her brow furrows. "What happened out there?"

I wince. Of course she's seen it. While she often opts not to watch in person, claiming it's too difficult to refrain from getting in the ring to defend me any time I take a hit, I forget that she watches every time without fail. Being married to Dad throughout his career, she knows MMA almost as well as he does. She knows I fucked up.

"I let something get into my head," I admit, shifting restlessly from one foot to the other. "It messed with me, and I was distracted."

"What?" she asks, eyeing me expectantly.

"Uh..." Time to admit the truth. "Sydney was there with a guy."

"*Oh.*" There's a wealth of meaning in the word. "A date?"

"Yeah." I squirm, wishing more than anything that I didn't have to have this talk.

"And that upset you because you have feelings for her." It's a statement, not a question. Mama's always been uncannily good at reading between the lines. Her expression softens. "Oh, Gabriel. I'm sorry."

"It's okay." I just want this over. "We're actually, uh, giving it a shot. Sydney and me. We're together now."

A thousand-watt smile lights her face. "*Felicidades!* Congratulations. That's the best news you could have given me. I'm so happy for you."

Huh. I scan her delicate features. Where's the shock? The concern? She knows this isn't a good time for me to be beginning a relationship.

"You aren't... surprised?" I ask.

She rolls her eyes. "Children think their parents see nothing, but we see it all. I knew you and Sydney would come together eventually. You've been circling each other for years."

"Oh." I deflate a little. All this time I thought I'd hidden my feelings, but it seems everyone knew all along. Jase did. Mama, too. Does Dad?

At the thought of confessing what's going on to him, a sliver of doubt penetrates the back of my mind. He's not going to take this as well as Mama, that's for sure.

"I guess it just took time for us to realize it."

She nods, and slips an arm around me. "Come on, let's go break the news to your *papa*."

As expected, Dad's mood becomes grim as soon as I manage to get the words out.

"What are you thinking?" He stands and paces the room like a caged tiger. "Couldn't you wait just a few weeks until after the Ruby Knuckles? There's so much at stake. Your dreams are finally within reach, and you're risking it by making a play for a girl who'll still be around afterward?" He fists his hands and throws a shadow punch, then another—a common tactic of his when he's trying to rein in his temper. "If this ends badly, you might have ruined your only chance." He drops his fists and turns toward me, face flushed. "Why now? Are you trying to self-sabotage?"

"No." I do my best not to take his reaction personally. It's a less than ideal situation, and I can acknowledge that. "I just couldn't handle seeing Sydney with someone else. I know the timing is off, but if I'd waited, I might have missed out."

"Young people," he mutters. "So overdramatic."

"Now, now, Tomas," Mama says. "Everything in life can't be MMA."

Dad sighs. "Be more simple if it was." He runs a hand through hair that used to be the same shade as mine but is now salt and pepper. "Just remember your priorities. You're with Sydney. You've got her. She's not going to meet another man before the Ruby Knuckles, so keep your eye on the prize. If your attention is off her for a little while, she'll understand. She's a good kid."

I'm not sure if she'll be as forgiving as he believes, but I'm grateful he hasn't flipped his lid, so I don't argue. I sink into an armchair. "Let's talk about the fight."

We debrief on the one with Taz Montgomery— although there isn't a lot to say other than that I fucked up, allowed myself to become distracted, and I won't let it happen again. After that, we switch to tactics for the upcoming fight. My opponent, Leo Delaney, is a solid fighter and I respect him. He has the misfortune of training out of the same gym as Karson Hayes, Lena's ex, but none of us hold Hayes's behavior against him.

We spitball ideas. Delaney is aggressive. He moves forward relentlessly. His style is the opposite of mine, but in this case, I think it'll work in my favor. So does Dad. He trained me to be a counter-fighter, and to use my brain, because he was a straight-up brawler and blames that for the head injury that ended his career.

He taught me to be different so I'd have more longevity. Right now, I'm thankful for it.

"You've got this," he says before I go, slinging an arm around me. "I know you'll do me proud, *mijo*. I'll see you later in the week."

"See you."

Mama waves. "*Te quiero mucho.* We love you."

On the journey home, I'm not sure how to feel. Talking to Dad unsettled me, although I'm not completely sure why or how. All I know is that I need to see Sydney as soon as I can, and unfortunately, it won't be until tomorrow.

Sydney

Thump. Thump. Thump.

My eyes open blearily, and I peer through my lashes at the clock. It's after six in the evening, but it's not uncommon for me to sleep for an entire day after a double shift.

Thump. Thump. Thump.

What is that infernal noise? It sounds like someone is bashing on the wall. My mind is foggy, but as the cobwebs clear, I realize they're knocking at my apartment door.

Strange, I wasn't expecting a visitor.

Dragging myself out of bed, I wrap a robe around my body to cover everything revealed by my tiny summer pajamas, then check that my overnight hair scarf is secure, and make my way to the door.

"Who is it?" I ask, standing on tiptoes to look through the peephole.

"It's Gabe. I have food." His voice is rough and

rumbly and sets my nerves alight something wicked. Now that I think about it, I do smell the delicious scent of spices. Curry, perhaps. But what's he doing here? Usually I celebrate if he turns up where he said he would at the appointed time without getting sidetracked along the way. "Are you going to let me in, Syd? Your neighbor is eyeballing me."

"Oh, yeah. Hold on a sec." Unlatching the door, I sigh at the sight of him. He's wearing jeans and a long-sleeved t-shirt that does great things for his body. My mouth waters, and I remember my own unkempt state. My first impulse is to hurry to the bedroom and fix myself up, but this is Gabe, and he's seen me in worse shape than this.

"Did I wake you?" he asks, pausing to drop a kiss on my forehead. For some reason, that simple, completely chaste action makes me feel more loved than any make-out session ever has.

"Yeah, but I was due to wake up anyway. If you give me ten minutes, I'll shower and join you for whatever it is that smells so delicious."

"Red Thai curry." He brushes past me into the apartment. "I'll dish some up and make you a coffee."

"God, you're wonderful." Taking his free hand in mine, I draw him close and kiss him properly.

His lips part and he growls against my mouth. "Don't tempt me, Syd, or I'll forget I came here with pure intentions."

Heat curls through me. "I wouldn't mind that."

But he's right, I should shower, so I pat his cute butt and head back to my bedroom, where I pull together a comfortable outfit. I'm in and out of the shower as quickly as possible, then I dress in my sweatpants and rejoin him in the living room. Two steaming bowls of curry sit side by side on the coffee table, with a mug of freshly brewed coffee beside one.

Inhaling deeply, I grin. "Seriously, the only way this could be better is if you were naked with tequila in your navel. Thank you."

His eyes darken. "That can be arranged."

I laugh. "Maybe after the Ruby Knuckles. Tomas would never forgive me if I corrupted you before then."

Something dark flashes across his face.

"That's probably true." His statement is more serious than warranted, which gives me pause, but then I notice his curry is untouched. He's clearly been waiting for me. Sweet, when I know how hungry he must be.

Grabbing the smaller bowl, I settle beside him and dig in. "Mm. This is so freaking good." As is the fact he's here and we didn't even arrange anything ahead of time. Dare I hope he's turning over a new leaf? "How was your day?"

"Long." He takes my cue and chows down on his dinner, absolutely decimating it. "Seth is killing me with cardio. He wants me to be able to go for as long as Leo can, in case I don't manage to win in the first couple of rounds."

"I'm sure you're just as fit as Leo. You've outlasted plenty of other fighters before." In fact, Gabe is famous for wearing people down. He isn't an out-and-out brawler like Jase or a whirlwind of insanity like Devon. Instead, he slowly and methodically breaks his opponents apart until they no longer have the willpower to fight back, then he moves in for the kill. I've seen it so many times, yet it never fails to electrify me.

"I won't know for sure until we're in the ring," he says, refusing to make any assumptions that might lessen his stress, in true Gabe fashion. The guy seems to like mentally beating himself up as a form of motivation. I suppose it's admirable, but I worry for him. At some point, he needs to just be happy with himself and what he's achieved. He can't keep living for someone else. And heck, maybe he'd make the exact same decisions if he wasn't motivated by his father, but I don't know that for certain, and it bothers me.

"How about you?" he asks. "Tell me about your shift."

I shrug. "Not much to tell. The usual accidents, falls, and crashes. I worked a double to cover for Ken, then came home and slept right through until you knocked on the door."

This feels nice, discussing our days. I hope it's the beginning of a new pattern. As friends, we've always just picked up where we left off, regardless of how much time had passed since we saw each other last, but this feels like a deeper connection. Something more intimate. That's how I want things to be with him.

Gabe drops his fork and wipes his mouth on a napkin. "So," he says. "I'm curious. I admitted that I've wanted you ever since I walked in on... you know." He gives me a meaningful look, and I blush, recalling the incident vividly. I couldn't look him in the eye for a week afterward. "It's only fair that you tell me how long you've seen me as more than a friend."

"Why do you want to know?" My insides clench at the thought of admitting how long I've lusted after him. I'm not sure I'm ready to be that honest yet. It's a little embarrassing.

He glances down, fidgeting uncomfortably. "It'd be nice to know I wasn't suffering alone."

"Is it enough to say you weren't?"

He shakes his head. "Fess up. It's your turn."

I wonder how to phrase this. The truth is mortifying, but we shouldn't start out a new relationship with falsehoods.

"High school," I squeak. "Sam Calder made fun of my hair and you broke his nose. I had just the tiniest crush on you after that."

"Oh, really?" He bares his teeth. "Me beating people up for you, that gets you going?"

"Not exactly. More like the fact you jumped to my defense without hesitation. Then Jenna Douglas dumped you over it and I felt so bad. She accused me of having feelings for you, and I couldn't deny it."

He shrugs. "She told me it was you or her, and there was no contest. I didn't even like her that much. I was just a horny kid who wanted whatever girl I could talk into bed with me."

I roll my eyes. "You weren't like that. You were a serial monogamist." I'd watched the stream of girls come and go, and meanwhile I'd dated other guys often enough to make sure I never raised his suspicions.

"Well, yeah. I wasn't gonna screw around on anyone, but I wasn't exactly choosy about who I dated, either."

Yet he'd never dated me. I suppose I should be flattered that he considered our friendship too important to mess with, but try convincing my ego of that.

"So what you're telling me," he says, starting on his curry again, "is that we could have been having fantastic sex for years, but we were both too scared to make a move?"

"Maybe," I admit. "But would it have been so

fantastic without a couple of decades of friendship behind it?" I feel like our closeness definitely impacts the quality of the sex.

"Guess we'll never know." He finishes his curry and looks at me in a way that's full of dark intent. Suddenly, I'm not hungry anymore. "But baby, this conversation has brought back memories that I don't like, and we need to fix that. I want you naked and coming on my cock. Is that good with you?" The last phrase comes out all growly, and holy shit I'm so turned on by the grating need in his voice that the slightest of touches could send me over the edge.

I whimper. "Uh, yes please." As if I'd say anything else. I strip my pants off. By the time I kick them away, Gabe's dick is out, and he's encircling it with his fingers, stroking languidly. I straddle him and his hands fall away. Rocking my hips back and forth, my pussy glides over him. I love his hardness and the way his teeth grit together as though he's struggling to contain himself.

"I want you in me," I say. "Make me forget anyone else."

Who cares about foreplay? I'm already soaked.

He hesitates. "Condoms."

"In the bedroom." I really wish we didn't have to use them though. That I could just sink onto him and feel us together skin to skin. I'm on birth control, and I'm clean. I assume he is too, but it's better safe than sorry.

"Get them."

Reluctantly, I break away from him and go to the bedroom, where I grab one from my bedside cabinet, then hurry back and pass him the foil packet. He tears it open and rolls it on, then lifts me over him, my knees outside his thighs. Slowly, I lower myself down, and he throws his head back, closing his eyes, his teeth clenched and fists balled at his sides. The cords of his neck stand out. I bite my lip. He's the hottest thing I've ever seen. When he's fully inside me, I start to ride him. Immediately, his fingers sink deeper into the soft flesh of my hips.

"Oh fuck, Syd. I'd forgotten how good you feel."

"How good *we* feel," I correct, dragging myself along his body, drowning in the bliss of friction in all the right places. My hands go to his chest, and I use him to hold myself up as I bounce on him the way he asked. His fingers journey around to my ass and knead it.

"Shit." His head rocks forward, and he licks my throat, then sucks. "Fuck," he murmurs against the skin, and looks up at me, dark eyes glittering. "If I ever see you doing this with anyone else again," he takes a moment to collect himself, the lines of his face taut with pleasure, "I'm gonna fuck him up so bad. You're mine now, baby. Only mine. *Always* mine."

Shivers race across my skin at his possessive words —the good kind—and my pussy clenches around him. It shouldn't turn me on, him threatening other guys, but I must be just as messed up as him because I love it. I love what it says about the strength of his feelings for me.

"Gabe," I whisper, staring into his eyes, maintaining a soul-deep connection. "What's happening with us?"

He drives up hard into me. "I don't know, but I never want it to stop. You're part of me, now. The best part." He lodges deeper, and I fall apart in his arms. He holds me tighter, his hips bucking. "Yeah, just like that. Let me know how good it feels. Oh, *fuck*." He growls into my neck, and I feel him jerk as he finds his bliss. When he stills, I rest my head on his shoulder while we catch our breath and my heart slows to its usual pace.

He weaves his fingers between mine. "Wanna come dancing on Friday? I want to take you out like you deserve."

I laugh, unsure where the question came from, but I'm totally down for it. I haven't gone dancing in months. "Count me in."

13

GABE

Inviting Sydney to go dancing was an impulsive idea. One I heartily regret. I wanted to give her something special, a night that would be out of the ordinary for us and cement our new status as a couple. I stand by that sentiment, but in between exercise, sparring, talking strategy with Dad and Seth, and making time to see her, when Friday rolls around, I'm dead on my feet. I'd much rather have a quiet night in, preferably napping on the sofa with my arms around my girl, but she's already messaged several times today, and I know how much she's looking forward to our outing. I can't let her down.

So instead of calling my chef and requesting dinner for two, I heat a meal from the freezer and eat alone, then dress in club-appropriate attire and take a cab to Sydney's place. I'm later than I said I would be because training went longer than expected, but at least I texted to let her know, so hopefully she isn't too upset. When she lets me in, she's looking sexier than ever in a black dress that stops at mid-thigh and leaves a lot of important places bare.

"Only an hour and a half late." A ghost of a smile plays at the corners of her mouth. "Thanks for the heads-up."

I study her expression, looking for an indication of her mood, but it's neutral. "Sorry, Seth wanted me to practice takedowns."

"That's okay." She shrugs. "I appreciate you messaging."

Cautiously, I bend and kiss her, hoping she won't turn away. She doesn't, thank God. "You look beautiful. You're going to be the death of me, dressed like that."

She brightens and performs a pirouette, her hair swirling around her face, dark eyes glittering. "You like it?"

"Hell, yes." Especially the way the fabric clings to her curves. Her body is dynamite, and there's nothing I want more than to get my hands on her. But tonight isn't about me, it's about her. About *us*. I've already screwed up enough by being late, reminding her of why she was reluctant to give me a chance in the first place. "Are you ready to go? I have a taxi waiting outside to take us to Flashlight, if that works for you." Flashlight is the most exclusive club in town.

Her eyes light up, and my lateness seems forgotten. "Do you think they'll let us in?"

I resist the urge to roll my eyes. "Between my net worth and public stature, I think we'll be okay."

She shakes her head, her smile wry. "I forget about that sometimes. To me, you're just my Gabe."

That's what I love about her. I'm a person, not an opportunity, or a legacy, or whatever else people see when they look at me. *Love.* I turn the word over in my mind. I do love her. Have for years. But I'm in danger of loving her in the deepest way possible, and while I'll never admit it, I'm worried this won't be the last time I'm late or a no-show, giving her a reason to doubt me. It seems inevitable.

"I'll just get my ID." She hurries into her room and returns a moment later, sliding something into her bra. *Jesus*, is that where modern women store things? "Come on." Impatiently, she tugs me to the door. I cast a longing look over my shoulder at her sofa, and then follow her out.

The drive takes a while because of traffic, but I manage to keep my hands to myself—mostly. When we arrive, I tuck Sydney under my arm and pass the line lingering outside the entrance, nodding to the bouncer, who waves me through without any fuss. I glance down at Sydney. Her eyes are wide.

"Wow, talk about special treatment. I'd have had to line up for hours if you weren't here."

"Perks of the job." Guilt sinks its claws into me because I haven't taken her out more often. This is something we should have done together, even as friends, isn't it? "Want a drink?"

"Nuh-uh. I want to dance." Taking my hand, she pulls me into the crowd of gyrating people.

Despite not being the kind of guy who's at home on the dance floor, I can hold my own. Growing up in a boxing ring means I'm light on my feet, and I'm easily the most graceful pro fighter at Crown MMA Gym—a badge I wear with honor. It makes me lethal. I whirl Sydney around, catching her by surprise, and adore the flash of teeth between her lips as she grins.

We dance, and I take full advantage of the opportunity to touch her, running my hands over the outline of her body, snagging my fingers in her hair, which she must have straightened because it falls in a veil over her shoulders and moves with her as she sways. So goddamn erotic. The air between us sizzles with tension, and I know she feels it every bit as much as I do because her pupils are enormous.

At one point, she excuses herself to go to the ladies' room and I slip to the edge of the crowd to wait, brushing off a couple of women who approach. When she emerges, I track her progress across the room, eyes narrowing when some douche in a white suit grabs her arm, stopping her. She says something and tries to shake him off, but he doesn't let go.

Scowling, I stride toward them and I'm at her side in an instant. "Is there a problem here?"

The douche has a friend with him, and the guy clearly recognizes me. Unlike the douche himself, who glances my way dismissively. "Excuse me, pal, I'm trying to talk to the lady."

"She's with me."

"I am." Sydney nods firmly, but can't detach from him because he's still gripping her tightly enough to cut off her circulation. If he doesn't release her within the next ten seconds, I'm going to be really pissed.

"Dude, that's Gabe Mendoza," the douche's friend hisses. "Let her go."

The guy's brows wrinkle in confusion. "Who?"

His friend edges closer, and tugs his hand clear of Sydney, who immediately huddles into my side. "Pro cage fighter. You don't want to mess with him."

"He's right," I warn. "You don't." Because seeing him manhandle her like that has me bristling for a fight. But the guy just shakes his head and mutters something about the chick not being worth it, and wanders off.

Sydney cocks her head, studying me with interest. "You're hot when you go all caveman."

A smile twists my mouth. "Is that so?"

She nods affirmatively. "Dance with me, caveman."

Letting her lead me back into the throng of dancers, I frown when spots dance in front of my eyes and my field of vision narrows. The world tilts on its axis, but a moment later, it rights itself.

Weird, what was that?

And who turned the temperature up? Because all of a sudden, I'm sweating like crazy. In fact, I feel like I've had a few too many drinks, when I haven't touched alcohol in weeks.

Shaking my head, I try to dispel the heaviness descending on me. Sydney is having a blast, and that's what matters. The feeling won't leave, but I can handle it. Especially when being here with her, and being allowed to touch her, is more than I ever dreamed of. A slow song starts, and we rock in time to it. Hands resting on her hips, I hold onto her when my head spins, using her as my rock. She doesn't seem to notice, laying her cheek on my chest. I press a kiss to the top of her head and inhale the scent of her.

I'm so blessed to have this woman as my best friend and my lover. And if I have anything to do with it, she'll have no reason to regret making more room for me in her heart.

14

SYDNEY

I wake wearing a smile. I've never done that before. But then, opening my eyes to see Gabe Mendoza's gorgeous face and hella sexy body in my bed isn't something I've done until recently, either. I suspect the two are correlated. Touching his shoulder, I trace the outline of his deltoid and kiss the muscle, then I wiggle closer and kiss his stubbly cheek.

"Gabe, wake up."

He doesn't stir, so I reach between us and wrap my fingers around his dick.

Still nothing.

Frowning, I brush another kiss over his lips and shift into a seated position. His head lolls to the side, and his mouth falls open, emitting a snore. I laugh. He's fast asleep. But it's growing light outside and I know he likes to exercise in the mornings, so I jostle his shoulder more firmly.

"Come on, baby. It's morning."

"Don't wanna," he groans, his lashes fluttering but eyes refusing to open. He rolls over, his head landing in my lap, and snuggles up close. My heart goes crazy. He's the cutest thing. An overgrown man-child with bulging biceps and a stubborn set to his chin.

"You've got to," I remind him, dropping a kiss on his forehead. "Seth will be expecting you at the gym."

"Ugh, fine." He sits up and spears his fingers through his hair, blinking blearily. "You're a hard woman, Sydney Coleman."

My lips quirk. "Don't you forget it."

Slowly, he extracts himself from the blankets. When he stands, he sways a little, and I wrap my arms around him to steady him.

"Are you okay? You didn't have anything to drink last night, did you?"

"Not a drop," he promises. "You know I don't do that during fight camp. I just had a really deep sleep and I'm still waking up."

"All right, then." I watch as he finds a clean pair of shorts and pulls a t-shirt over his head. I can't quite put my finger on it, but something feels off about him.

"Are you sure you're fine?" I ask, following him into the kitchen.

He starts fixing breakfast and one corner of his mouth hooks up. "Never better, *cariño*."

He switches the blender on and for a moment, all we can hear is the whir of blades, then he turns it off and chugs a mouthful of his smoothie. I can't help but notice he's a little pale, but when I cross to him and touch the back of my hand to his forehead, he doesn't have a fever.

His eyes twinkle. "Am I too hot?"

"For my sanity." My hand drops to my side and I try to shake off the sense that something is wrong. It's probably just that I'm scared to relax and enjoy myself now everything is going well.

Yeah, that must be it.

If only I could believe it.

GABE

My head is pounding like crazy, but I don't let on to Sydney as she prepares her own smoothie. I've clued into the fact that I've probably overdone things this week, but surely this mammoth headache is overkill. After all, it's not like I've gone completely over the top. Other people manage to be championship fighters while maintaining happy relationships. Hell, just look at Jase and Lena, and Jase didn't have the advantage of being raised by a Ruby Knuckles finalist. I should be able to handle this.

Sydney's eyes widen as I drink. "Whoa. Don't forget to breathe."

I give her my cockiest grin, and say, "Breathing is for wimps."

She rolls her eyes as I drain the rest of my drink. I place the mug in the sink and wipe my mouth on a napkin, then give her one more kiss and get out of there before she asks any more questions. Sydney can be stubborn as hell when she wants to be. I catch a taxi home, then grab my training gear and drive to the gym. Music is blaring as I toss my bag over my shoulder and head in.

"You're late," Seth grunts as I enter. He's holding pads for one of the newer guys, Jimmy something-or-other, and looks up just long enough to give me a withering stare of disapproval. My balls try to crawl up inside me. Seth is scary as hell sometimes.

"Sorry, man. Won't happen again." I'm not the type to offer excuses or useless explanations.

"Better not." He nods toward the skipping ropes. "Warm up, do a hundred burpees so you remember the importance of being punctual, then we'll do King of the Ring. You, Dev, and Jase can show young Jimmy here what it takes to be the best."

"Got it." I wrap my hands, then grab a skipping rope from a hanger on the wall and start jumping. When my body is warm, I transition to burpees—or as I like to call them, the Devil's exercise. I don't know what it is, maybe just the fact I'm bigger than any of the other guys here, but it takes me twice as long to do burpees as everyone else, and I expend twice as much effort. Simply put, all the guys here have a weakness, and they're mine. Seth knows it too, the sadistic bastard. My vision swims as I leap up and down, and several times I don't get my hands out fast enough to avoid body slamming the floor.

Jesus, what's wrong with me today?

Finally, I finish, and Seth calls me straight over to the ring, where the other guys are lined up and leaning on the ropes.

"Dev and Jase," he says. "Show Jimmy what Crown MMA fighters are made of. First one to land a clean shot or take their opponent to the floor stays in, the loser subs out." He turns to me. "I want you talking Jimmy through this. He kicked ass in the amateurs, but he's playing with the big boys now, and you're going to be the helping hand guiding him into the pros." He leans closer and murmurs in my ear, "We want some of the cockiness knocked out of him, but not all of it."

I nod, knowing exactly what he means. Fighting takes confidence, but too much can be deadly if there's nothing to back it up. I offer Jimmy a fist, and he bumps it. He's a lean white kid, perhaps twenty or so, with hooded blue eyes and a half-smirk. I don't know where Seth recruited him from, but I have a feeling he's about to go through the MMA equivalent of hazing.

Devon and Jase step into the center of the ring, circling each other, then Devon strikes, quick as a snake, throwing a jab as a decoy before launching an uppercut at the underside of Jase's chin. But for all that Devon is fast, Jase has been doing this for longer, and he dodges out of the way and kicks at Devon's ankle, trying to take him down. Dancing out of reach, Devon circles back with a push kick aimed at Jase's solar plexus. It lands, but Jase hardly reacts, so Seth doesn't call the round. They continue going at it until Devon throws a suicidal head kick. I say suicidal because it's exactly the opportunity Jase needs to sweep his remaining leg out from under him and tackle him to the floor.

Seth blows his whistle, and Devon groans. "Damn it, one of these days I'm gonna get you."

"My turn," Jimmy says, swaggering forward to face Jase, who's grinning in a way that makes me nervous for what's about to come. At least it's Jase in the ring with the kid rather than Devon, who doesn't know how to take it easy.

"Don't let him get you on the ground," I tell Jimmy. "He'll try to sweep your legs out or get you off balance. Don't be too heavy on your feet or you're a goner."

He nods, raising his hands to protect his jaw, but I can see he isn't taking this as seriously as he should be. Jase isn't going to go easy on him, although he won't knock the kid hard enough to put him out of commission. That would just piss Seth off. It's a shame I don't know more about Jimmy's style, because I don't know which moves come naturally to him.

He throws a quick jab-cross combo and ends with a low kick. Jase blocks the punches and checks the kick. He's going slow, feeling the new boy out and lulling him into a false sense of security. It's working, too. Jimmy comes forward more aggressively, throwing another jab, which Jase parries, followed by an overhand right. I see the gleam in Jase's eye, and then he slips the punch and drives up with his knee, directly into Jimmy's solar plexus. The kid goes down, gasping. I hurry over and grab his arms, raising them above his head so he can breathe more easily.

"Fuck," he wheezes. "What was that?"

"That was me proving I'm more than a brawler," Jase remarks. "Wise up, man. Just because you only see me rolling around the ring, that doesn't mean I'm shit as a stand-up fighter."

The kid nods, still dragging in air. "Got it."

"Jimmy, out," Seth barks. "Gabe, you're with Jase. How about bringing this cocky mofo down a peg?"

"On it, boss." I pop my mouthguard in and step forward as Jimmy flops out of the ring. He's not down for good though—I can see from his expression that the setback has only made him hungry for more, which is the kind of attitude it takes to survive around here.

Jase and I face each other as we have a thousand times before. I know his style so well that I can see what he's going to do before he takes more than a couple of steps. The first strikes set the tone, and if I can keep him at a distance, I've got him. He knows this, so he charges. Unfortunately, even though I see it coming, my reflexes are slow. It takes me half a second too long to get out of the way, and that's all he needs to tackle me to the ground. The moment we're down, he sits up, straddling me, staying in position long enough to let me know he won the round.

Seth growls in disgust. "Slow, Gabe. Too fucking slow."

"Yeah, I know." Sighing, I tag out as Devon tags in. This time, Devon goes balls to the wall, and utilizes his full speed and reach advantage to throw a barrage of strikes at Jase that have him veering back. An uppercut lands, and Jase bumps gloves with Devon and nods, acknowledging a strike well done. The new boy looks a little sickly, so I replace Jase and spar with Devon. Usually, we're a good match—where he's aggressive, I'm thoughtful—but today my timing is off and I can't dodge, block, and redirect with my usual efficiency. When one of his solid right-hand punches land, it's hard enough to rattle me.

"My bad," he exclaims. "Sorry, man. Thought you had that, for sure."

"So did I," I grumble.

"What's with you today?" he asks. "You're off your game."

"Gabe, get over here," Seth snaps, before I can answer. I go to him. His green eyes are blazing. "You've been doing this for too long not to know what's responsible when you're having a shit time at training. So whatever it is, deal with it, and come back tomorrow in better form."

I gape. "You're sending me home? But it was only a couple of missed counters."

He gives me a look that says he isn't falling for my bullshit. "You and I both know better than that. Sort it out."

"Oooh," Devon mutters, "you got told."

"Is he always like that?" Jimmy asks, loud enough that everyone cringes.

I stop as I pass him and lower my voice to reply. "He's tough, but fair, and that's what makes this the best place to train." I offer him a hand up. "Come on, give it another shot. This time, aim for Jase's right thigh. The fucker doesn't condition it properly."

Nodding, he thanks me, and heads back into the ring. I don't bother supervising because Jase made his point, and I trust him to take things easier from here on out.

"What's going on?" Devon asks softly.

Sighing, I shrug my shoulders, trying to ease some of the tension that's built in them. "Went dancing with Syd last night. Didn't handle it so well. Need a good rest."

He shakes his head. "You've got to take care of yourself. You're always the first guy to tell us not to go out partying in the lead-up to a big fight, so why aren't you taking your own advice?"

He has a point, but it isn't that simple. Not this time.

"I've only just convinced Sydney to give me a shot. If I start bailing out of things already, she'll wash her hands of me."

His brow shoots up. "You really think so? Because from the cheap seats, Syd seems like a pretty reasonable woman. Plus she understands what this means to you, and what's involved in getting the W, more than most people."

I grunt, because he's right, she does understand the massive amount of work we put in. But then, she also knew that when she told me not to bother being with her unless I was committed to making time for us.

"All I'm saying is, talk to her. See what happens. If you need another opinion, ask your Dad for advice. Him and your mom must have been through all this and they managed to pull through."

I shake my head. Talking to Dad about Sydney right now doesn't seem like the best choice, and nor does being open with her about where I'm at. "Thanks, anyway. Can I ask you something?"

"Of course, brother."

"If you have all the answers, then where's your girl?"

He snorts with laughter and backs away from me, in the direction of the ring. "I have all the answers, so I know that a girl isn't in the cards for me yet. When she is, you can bet your sweet ass that I'll talk about my damn feelings with her."

He turns and leaps into the cage, leaving me to wonder if he's onto something, and also why I'm considering taking advice from my playboy buddy.

15

SYDNEY

Gabe messages to let me know he's gone home to rest under Seth's orders, and after praising the universe for his coach being an unusually insightful guy, I drop by later in the day to check on him. As I let myself in, I can't help but wonder if his tiredness is my fault. We've had the most perfect week together, but have I asked too much of him? I know he's got a lot going on and I hate the thought that my selfish desire to spend time with him might have worn him out.

"Hey, Gabe," I call, removing my shoes.

No reply.

I pad through rooms, checking for any sign of him. His house is something of a mansion. Big and expensive, but comfortable too. He's not the show-pony type, so all of the furniture is soft and welcoming, and his mother and I helped choose the color scheme, which consists of warm neutral shades. It's a home designed for living, and I love it. When he first had the place built, he offered me one of the rooms for a ridiculously low rent, but I didn't want to take advantage of his generosity. On top of that, I've secretly fantasized about him for years. Who wants to live with their best-friend-slash-crush? That's just inviting disaster. Either I'd have done something to expose my feelings, or been devastated any time he brought a girl home.

Of course, I view it differently now. Except for the work situation, there's no reason I wouldn't want to live here with him—as his girlfriend. Smiling at the thought, I knock on his bedroom door, then ease it open. He's sprawled across his bed, face down, and fast asleep.

Good. He needs his rest.

But he's too tempting to just leave there, so I climb onto the bed beside him and get swallowed by the cocoon of his body as he wraps an arm around me and pulls me close. Shutting my eyes, wrapped in the scent of him, I drift into a dream.

When I wake, it's two hours later and he's still sleeping. I debate whether to wake him up or leave him, but if he sleeps all afternoon then he won't at night, so I smooth his hair back and talk to him softly.

"Wake up, Gabe. Nap time is over."

He doesn't respond. Perhaps he's really out of it, like he was earlier.

I squeeze his shoulder. "Come on, big guy."

He doesn't react, and my heart starts to hammer. This isn't normal. Gabe is not a deep sleeper. Something's wrong beyond a little overtiredness.

"Wake up." I lower my ear to his chest and hear a solid whump-whump-whump, which doesn't ease my anxiety as much as I'd like. Grabbing my phone, I switch the flashlight app on and aim the light at his face.

He turns away, groaning. "What are you doing?"

His voice is thick with sleep, but not slurred. A good sign.

"Bringing you back to the land of the living," I reply, aiming for levity but falling short. "How are you feeling? Do you have a headache?"

"Hurts like a bitch. Might be a migraine."

I get to my feet. "I'll get you an aspirin and a glass of water, then we're going to the doctor."

In the kitchen, I find a box of aspirin and extract two. I fill a glass of water and carry it back to him. He's sitting, propped against a pillow, and I pass him the pills and watch while he chugs them down and drains the entire glass.

"Thirsty?"

"A little." He sighs. "I don't need to see a doctor. It's no big deal. I'll be fine tomorrow."

My hand goes to my hip. "As a doctor, I say that's bull. We're going."

"Fine." He climbs out of bed. "We're taking my bike."

"Uh, no. We're not. We'll get an Uber." I already have my phone out, summoning up the app before he can argue.

Half an hour later, we're shown into the emergency doctor's office.

"What seems to be the problem?" she asks, tucking a loose lock of hair behind a delicate ear.

Gabe shrugs.

Rolling my eyes, I explain. "Headache, tiredness. He thinks it might be a migraine. Anything else, babe?"

He perks up at the endearment. "Trouble concentrating. A bit lethargic."

"Hmm, okay," the doctor murmurs as she jots a note.

"Do you mind if I measure your blood pressure and listen to your chest?"

"Go right ahead."

She does so, sliding a cuff onto his arm. He winces when she pumps it up.

"Your blood pressure is low," she remarks. "But that's not unusual for athletes." She checks his eyes and takes his temperature. "How long have you been experiencing symptoms?"

"Since last night."

Finally, she sets her tools down and looks at us. "I'd say we're dealing with a little fatigue. Nothing serious, but you need to get plenty of sleep over the next few days and not overdo things. Think you can manage that?"

I snort. Because Gabe, not overdo things? She's asking for the impossible.

But he simply nods and says, "Yeah, sure. Thanks, doc."

"I'll write you up for a blood test just to make sure." She scrawls something on a piece of paper, tears it off a pad, and passes it to him. "Take this next door. They'll get back to you within a few days, but I don't think you have anything to worry about."

He gives me a look as if to say, "See?"

I ignore him. "Thanks for your time." I stand, and he does, too. "Have a nice day."

As we leave, he reaches for my hand and tucks it inside his. Tingles shoot up my arm. "You worry too much, Syd. I just need a good sleep."

"At least now we know." Although if I'm being honest, I can't help the unsettling feeling that it's not that simple.

130

ON SUNDAY, after a sleep in for both of us, I linger in the doorway of Gabe's home gym, ogling him from behind while he does squats at a weight rack.

Damn boy, he looks fine.

I could happily incorporate this vision into my daily life. He squats down, his muscular butt sticking out, and I lick my lips. As he straightens, his powerful thighs bunch, and God, there is a whole lot to admire when it comes to Gabe Mendoza's body. From the swirling ink peeking out above his sneakers to the wall of muscle that is his chest, to his unwaveringly intense black gaze set in a brutally beautiful face. I've been watching him for signs of strain, or that he's not feeling recovered, but from all appearances, he's fine.

My phone rings, and his eyes dart to mine in the mirror, but he doesn't flinch, which suggests he knows I've been watching him all along. He doesn't smirk or play the peacock, as his friends might. He just keeps working, letting me look my fill. A shiver courses through me. I wonder if he'll want to check me out the same way later.

The phone rings again, and I glance at the caller ID. It's Mom. Turning away to answer, I walk out of hearing distance. I haven't told her about the recent twist in our relationship yet. But then, she's not the type to care much one way or the other except for the potential bragging rights.

"Hi, Mom." Pacing down the hall, I make my way to the living room, where I sit on a massive sofa and tuck my feet beneath me. I'm wearing one of Gabe's over-sized tees and nothing else. I feel way underdressed for the conversation that's sure to come. My cousin Christina's wedding is next weekend, and I RSVP'd with a plus one that I didn't have. I'd planned to find someone, or drag a friend along with me, and for once, my optimism has actually paid off.

"Hello, Sydney," she says, her voice buttery smooth. Mom is a singer. The classy type who specializes in jazz and theater, and she's always been disappointed I don't share her passion. Unfortunately, I'm completely tone-deaf—a constant letdown. "I hope you've remembered Christina's wedding. I trust I'll see you there."

"Yes, you will."

"With a date?" Her arch tone suggests I'd better not embarrass her by turning up stag to another family event. There's nothing that the Colemans enjoy more than gossiping, and as the spinster who ranks her career higher than marrying well, I'm an easy target. Most of my cousins are dancers. Beautiful, vivacious, and used to being the center of attention. When they get together, it's like a reunion of the cast of Mean Girls. And I'm the butt of their jokes. Mom doesn't discourage them, and after a lot of reflection, I've decided it's because she hopes they'll bully me into fixing what she perceives to be my flaws.

"Yes, mother, with a date." A smug smile curves my lips. Technically, I haven't asked Gabe to join me, but I'm sure he will. I know for a fact he has no plans next Saturday, and he's never made a secret of his poor opinion of my family so I'm sure he'll be happy to support me and counteract their disdain. Assuming he's feeling okay, of course. I'll be keeping an eye on him to make sure.

"Who?" For once in my life, she actually sounds interested.

"Gabe."

"Oh." Her tone is dismissive and I can sense her mood deflating down the line. "When you said a date, I thought you meant you're finally seeing someone."

With a shake of my head, I remind myself to be patient. She doesn't intend any ill will. We're simply different people. A little too different, perhaps.

"I am. Gabe and I are dating."

"Really?" Her excitement returns, and it frustrates me. I've always wanted to do something—anything—to please this woman, but at the end of the day, it isn't me who impresses her, it's the thought that I might have hooked a wealthy and famous athlete. "Has he finished sowing his wild oats and decided it's time to settle down?"

This makes me laugh despite myself. The thought that Gabe might have been sowing wild oats for the past few years is ridiculous. He's been too busy working his ass off in the gym.

"Sure, that's exactly it."

"Good. I'll see you both there. Don't forget to wear—"

"I'm not wearing black to a wedding," I interrupt. "But never fear, I'll make sure I'm appropriately attired." I may also slip a flask of tequila into my purse. It wouldn't be the first time I've needed one to get through a family event. "Say hi to Dad for me. Bye."

Ending the call, I head back to Gabe's home gym and almost walk into him coming the other way. Stopping abruptly a safe distance from his chest, I try not to stare. But really, he's too gorgeous, and it wouldn't be right not to appreciate the work he puts in.

"Who was that?" he asks, and brushes a kiss over my cheek.

"Mom." I pull a face. "Making sure I haven't

forgotten Christina's wedding and that I won't disgrace her with my appearance."

"Ugh, Christina." He mimics my expression. "Is she the one who invited herself into my apartment that time she stayed with you?"

"Don't remind me."

It was years ago, before Gabe could afford this place, and we lived in the same building. Christina and I went over to see him during one of her visits and she took something he said as a come-on and turned up on his bed later in the evening—naked. He kicked her out—sans clothes—and she's never fully recovered.

Some men might like to be surprised with a bare, willing woman in their bed, but not Gabe. That isn't his style, and damn if his quick dismissal of her didn't warm me on the inside. His entire approach to life and relationships lets me know that this thing between us is special and different. I'm not just another girl in his bed.

Heart in my throat, I ask, "Will you come with me?"

He hesitates for half a second, then nods. "Of course. You think I'd miss an opportunity to grope you in front of those hyenas you call cousins?"

Throwing my arms around him, I bury my face in his sweaty chest. "Thank you, thank you, thank you."

He wraps his arms around me, cradling me, holding me close. Despite his sweatiness, the embrace is oddly tender. "Anything for you, Syd."

Guilt pricks at my conscience. I shouldn't be putting pressure on him to go to social engagements like this wedding when it's only a few weeks until the Ruby Knuckles finale, but one night should be fine... right? Besides, there's no reason for my feelings and goals to rank beneath his.

I wish I were more certain of that.

Patting Sydney's back, I inhale the coconut scent of her hair and press my lips to her temple. I have no qualms about making this relationship public. As far as I'm concerned, it's been long enough coming. And while I don't really want to spend a night hanging out with her unpleasant family when I could be resting or researching my opponent, I'd do it ten times over for her.

Releasing her, I step back. "I have to go to training."

"Oh, okay." Her face falls, but only temporarily. "So you're feeling better?"

"Like brand new." It's a slight exaggeration, but I'm only a little worse for wear. Much better than yesterday.

"Do you mind if I hang out here for the day?" she continues. "It's so much nicer than my place, and I want to be here when you finish."

"Go right ahead." I'm going to be tortured by images of her lazing around my house in her underwear though. Resentment tears through me. I don't *want* to leave her just to go and punch a bag and tussle with my friends. I want to stay right here and talk to her, cuddle her, find out where she sees us going and what I can do to keep her happy. But I need to go. At times like this, training isn't optional. It's my job, and I'm paid damn well for it. Besides, with ten hours of sleep behind me, I don't have any excuse not to go.

"Oh, before I forget," she adds. "I have an evening shift tonight, so I'll wait to say hi, and then I'll have to head to work."

I sigh. It figures. This is why we've never seen each other as much as we'd like to—our schedules are incompatible. Her news only makes me more anxious to ditch the gym and spend the coming hours with her. Weird. Training usually takes priority over everything and that's never bothered me much before. It's the way I was raised. Is it possible that my priorities are shifting? Because for once, the thought of my upcoming fight is dragging me down, while the beautiful face smiling at me makes everything feel worthwhile.

I love you.

Is it too soon to say it?

We haven't been together long, but I've known her forever. Softly, I kiss her lips, holding her dark gaze, trying to tell her with my eyes how strong and pure my feelings for her are.

"I'll see you soon, *mi vida.*"

16

GABE

"Gabe," Seth says as I walk into the gym on Friday afternoon, the day before Sydney's cousin's wedding. I've just gotten off the phone with the medical laboratory, who confirmed my blood work looks normal, so that's one less thing on my mind. "I got something to talk to you about."

Uh-oh, this can't be good.

"What's up?" I ask, dumping my bag and pulling off my shoes. Dad is here, too, standing near Seth, who's leaning on the wall beside me with his arms crossed over his massive chest.

"Been contacted about an opportunity for you. Interested?" Seth asks.

I hoist my bag up and stow it in a locker. "Depends. What is it?"

Dad scowls. "What difference does it make? If he has an opportunity, you should say 'yes, coach.'"

Biting my tongue, I manage not to reply. Dad means well, and I shouldn't let him get to me. He's used to me prioritizing MMA over everything else, so it will take a while for him to adjust to me carving out a bigger place for Sydney in my life. Also, it's not as though he knows I've been struggling. I haven't mentioned the trip to the doctor because I didn't want to worry him.

I nod to Dad and ask Seth, "What is it?"

"Ricky DeSilva's opponent pulled out of his fight tomorrow night," he says. "They're looking for a replacement. You'll pick up an easy three grand for competing, and an extra twenty if you win."

My eyebrows knit together. "You want me to fight on a day's notice?"

He shrugs. "It's a short timeframe, hence the big win bonus." One of his hands falls on my shoulder, and he looks me straight in the eye, getting way too close into my personal space. "Come on, Gabe. You've been training hard, and you need a clean win after what happened during your last fight. Less than forty-eight hours and it'll be over."

He's swaying me, and he knows it.

"Do it, *mijo*," Dad urges. "It'll put you in a good headspace for the Ruby Knuckles. We've been working toward it for so long."

We.

That word choice is intentional. He wants me to remember how much sweat and tears he's put into getting me where I am. I owe it to him to win. I *want* to win for him.

"How long do I have to think on it?" I ask Seth.

"The promoter needs an answer by the end of today. Otherwise, they'll cancel. You're the only one who's available and ready. Seriously, I think you should do this."

He leaves me to prepare for training.

"There's no downside," Dad says, moving closer. "It's

win-win. A short commitment from you to get you back on track to where you want to be." He nods, and gives me a slight smile. "I know you can see that, so I'll let you get to it. See you tomorrow."

"Bye."

Once he leaves the gym, I sigh. It's no surprise that both Dad and Seth think I should do it. A couple of weeks ago, I'd have thought the same. But that's before I committed to Sydney.

Hell. Sydney.

The wedding is tomorrow night. If I accept this fight, I'll miss the ceremony, and probably the dinner too. I can't let her down when I promised I'd go with her.

As I wrap my hands, I mull it over. Leaving her hanging would be a dick move, especially when I know what her family is like, but much as I hate to admit it, Seth is right. Even though I came away with the win, my last fight was disastrous, and this matchup with Ricky would be a great way to prove to myself—and everyone else—that my head is in the game. Perhaps I can ask for the fight to happen early in the show, and then join her at the wedding after. Instantly, my mind rebels. I've been trying to take it easier since last weekend and don't want to wear myself out, but I can't really see another option. I send Sydney a text.

Gabe: *Been offered a fight tomorrow night.*

Half an hour later, after I've warmed up, I check my phone. No response. But she's on an evening shift, so maybe she's busy. Seth summons me for pad rounds and drills me through my best combos and counters until I'm bathed in sweat and it's literally dripping from the tips of my hair. When we finish, I guzzle water and check again. There's a response, and I click on it immediately.

Sydney: *With who?*

Gabe: *Ricky DeSilva.*

Sydney: *As if he'd have any chance against you. You're so out of his league. Besides, you've already beaten him before.*

This makes me smile. I love her faith in my ability. But is she encouraging me to do it? I can't tell. Perhaps she hasn't made the connection with the wedding yet.

Gabe: *Don't know what I should say. We've got Christina's wedding...*

Sydney: *I'm sure you'll do the right thing. You know Seth has always got your back, no matter what.*

Rolling my head from side to side, I stretch my neck and try to read the subtext. She isn't being helpful. I need a yes or no answer. I get her not wanting to tell me what to do, but surely she could offer an opinion, especially about something that affects both of us. Or maybe she's trying to, with that reference to Seth. He's the one who mentioned the fight, and she's not wrong when she says he's always got my back. But is she saying I should go for it? Who knows? I need more certainty.

Devon pulls up beside me. "Problems in paradise?"

I cock my head and consider talking to him about my dilemma, but this is a guy who's one hundred percent dedicated to MMA, and he won't understand. He'd just take the fight and try to charm Sydney into forgiving him later.

"Nothing major," I reply, putting my phone away. Jase would be a better option to talk to because he worships the ground Lena walks on, but he's always been more emotional than me and I'm not sure if following his lead is the best idea. So instead I keep all of the worry inside me and stew on it.

Sydney

When I arrive home from the evening shift, I collapse onto the sofa. Groaning, I kick my shoes off and knead the bottoms of my feet, which ache from being on them for hours. My stomach growls, but I can't handle the thought of standing up again so soon, so I rummage in my work bag and dig out a protein bar. It's dry in my mouth, but for now, it'll have to do. My water bottle is empty, so I have nothing to wash it down with. Once I manage to swallow, I rest my head on the arm of the sofa and close my eyes. I don't even care that I'm still dressed and haven't brushed my teeth. I just need to sleep. Exhaustion creeps over me and I'm drifting in that peaceful state between slumber and wakefulness when a shrill screech frightens me back to full consciousness.

My phone. I glare at it, then snatch up the offending device and squint at the screen. It's Gabe again. He probably wants to talk about that fight he was offered. It's been on my mind ever since he messaged. I know turning it down won't have been easy for him, but surely he knows it was the best thing to do. He promised he'd be at the wedding for me, and he knows how much it means. How awful the women in my family can be.

Besides, he's supposed to be taking it easy. Not over-doing things. I didn't want to come right out and tell him to turn it down because I don't want to be *that* girl-friend, but with how many reasons there are *not* to do it, I'm confident he'll have made the right choice. Ricky DeSilva is no challenge for him anyway. Been there, done that. Why bother facing him again? I mean, if it had been years, sure, but Gabe faced him only a few months ago.

Sighing, I hit answer. "Hi, Gabe."

"Hey." His voice is strained, and I sit up straighter. "Did I wake you?"

"Yeah, kinda, but it's okay." Why did I say that? My sleep is valuable. But then, I suppose if he's calling now, it must be important. He knows I need rest after a shift like the one I just did.

"Can we talk about the fight?"

Knew it. "Sure thing."

"What do you want me to do about it?"

I press a hand to my abdomen, my heart shrinking in my chest. If he's asking me, it means he hasn't turned it down. And that means, despite everything, he wants to do it. But honestly, what does he expect me to say? No, you can't? You should go to the wedding with me like you promised you would?

That's not the kind of person I am. Much as I hate it, I want him to do whatever makes him happy. I just wish that were something with me. Because let's be real, if he can't even survive a couple of weeks as part of a functioning couple, what future do we have?

And that's not mentioning his health. I know he thinks he's fine, but he's in a precarious place, and needlessly taking on something as intense as this will be hard for him.

Ugh, I'm too tired to deal with this crap.

"What do you want to do?" I ask, because I'm not letting him make me the villain here.

"Well," he says slowly, as though trying to hedge his bets, "it's a great opportunity, and if I got the fight shifted to earlier in the evening, I might be able to make it for some of the wedding."

Sighing, I yank a hand through my hair. He's trying, I'll give him that. He's been trying for the past couple weeks, and except for being late once or twice, everything is going really well. But some contrary part of me doesn't want to make this easy for him. I want him to prove he took it seriously when he promised to give us a proper chance. I want him to prioritize something other than MMA and living out his Dad's dream.

"I already RSVP'd for dinner at the reception. Do you think you could make it by then?"

His silence is answer enough. Of course he couldn't. These events often don't begin until after dark and they're not going to risk putting him on too early in the night in case people miss out.

"Syd—"

"No," I interrupt, frustrated both with myself and with him. Why did I ever think he could change? I shake my head. If he wants an easy out, then he came to the wrong place. "You told me you'd be there. Are you seriously going to blow me off for a rematch against a guy we both know you can destroy?"

"That's not what I'm doing. I need to get my mojo back, and it's just one night."

I hate how calm he sounds, and his words are like a spear to the gut. *Just one night*? Does he truly not understand how much his support would mean to me? It may be only one night, but it's rare that I'm forced to spend time with my family. And okay, it's not like they're evil, but they just don't *get* me, and when I'm around them, I feel small and insignificant.

Suddenly, I'm weary, and just so fucking tired of being put on hold. My head is pounding and I need to sleep. "It's more than that, and you know it. But if you feel like you need this fight, then don't let me stop you.

Just do it. We both know you'll make the decision you think will make Tomas happy, regardless of anything else. I'm sorry, but I really need to get back to sleep now."

"Syd—"

With a forceful jab of the screen, I end the call. I'm not surprised when he rings again immediately. I reject it and send a text.

Sydney: *Just do it. I'll be fine.*

After all, I always am. It isn't the first time he's let me down, and I'm sure it won't be the last. I curl up and tears trickle down my cheeks, soaking into the sofa. With a trembling hand, I message Lena.

Sydney: *I need a hot date for a wedding tomorrow night. You free?*

Her reply is instantaneous.

Lena: *Absolutely. Need Jase to beat someone up for you?*

Sniffing, I wipe my eyes. Thank God for girlfriends.

Sydney: *No. Just wear the blue dress. I want the hottest girl there on my arm.*

Lena: *You got it, babe. XO*

17

GABE

I look up from my phone, which is connected to the livestream playing via the stadium's audiovisual system, as Dad enters the white-walled room and closes the door with a snick. On my phone screen, the first fighters of the night are circling in the ring.

"You spoke to Darius?" I ask. Darius is the guy responsible for the event.

"Yeah. He's changed you to fight number six. Couldn't get him to go any earlier."

I nod. I know he would've done the best he could. "Thanks."

Sydney may have told me not to bother coming to the wedding, but I still intend to be there as soon as I can. My suit is hanging against the wall, waiting for me to change into it once the fight is over.

"Let's wrap your hands," Seth says, dragging a chair over to sit opposite me, then straddling it backward. I lay my phone on the bench beside me, and out of the corner of my eye, I see Jase, Devon, and Dad bend over it to watch the action. They stay quiet, knowing that silence is what I need to get into the right headspace.

Meanwhile, Seth starts wrapping my hands and murmurs, "You made a good choice. You're ready for this, and you're gonna kill Ricky tonight. You've got it in the bag. Just do what you've trained to. Go in slow, don't let him rush you, and pick him apart like you do best. You need this win, Gabe."

He's right, I do, which is why I ultimately decided to take the fight. I'll have plenty of opportunities to make things up with Sydney, but I'm at a once-in-a-lifetime point in my career and if this is what it takes to get me back on track, then it's what I have to do.

"I got it," I said. "He's going down."

Seth nods, and we remain quiet while he finishes with my hands, then I skip for a few minutes to warm up, and stretch. The boys lay a towel on the ground and I lie on it while a physiotherapist rubs my muscles with a combination of liniments that will keep me warm and supple. The familiar scent helps me focus. Once I'm done, Jase hands me a pair of padded gloves and dons another set himself. We don't fight in these—we'd look ridiculous—but they ensure I won't get seriously hurt while we spar beforehand.

Jase and I fall into a rhythm. The sparring is intended to get me in the zone, get my limbs moving in the correct ways, and perhaps most importantly, get rid of the shock factor when the first strike lands in the octagon. That's a dangerous time, because too many people let that first punch or kick shake them, and once they're on the back foot, it's nearly impossible to recover.

Jase and I circle, and he comes forward aggressively, trying to mimic Ricky's fighting style. Ricky is from the "never take a backward step" school of thinking, whereas I've found that sometimes a sly and strategic retreat is the key to winning. He strikes and I slip out of the way and counter with a kick. He lurches forward and I plant my foot above his diaphragm and push. The breath wheezes from his lungs, but he doesn't let up, keeping the pressure on. After a couple of minutes, Seth separates us, and Jase swaps places with Devon, who doesn't have to pretend to be crazy aggressive because that's his natural state. He throws wacky combinations that many martial artists would shake their head over, but somehow he makes them work. I suspect it's because he has an innate sense of balance and timing that allows him to move like a fucking cat. He has nine lives like one, too. As he charges, I dance out of the way and hit back with a counterstrike. We go on like this for only thirty seconds or so, by which time sweat is beading on my hairline and Seth is satisfied that I'm ready for battle.

"Kick ass, bro," Jase says as a messenger comes to collect us. It's nearly go-time.

"You got this, *mijo*," Dad adds.

Seth settles our gym's robe over my shoulders and double-checks the items in his bucket. "Stay calm, and break him."

"Embrace your inner psycho," Devon advises with a maniacal grin. Somehow, I think his advice is the least helpful.

Rolling my eyes, I follow Seth to a door that separates the back rooms from the stadium. I can hear the crowd, but I tune them out, counting my breaths. My music starts to play—a death metal song that always gets me pumped—cuing my entry, and I stride out, staring straight ahead at the cage. The audience doesn't matter. I'm here to prove something to myself, to Seth, and to my next opponent, then I'm gonna get out of here and track down my girl. At the cage, someone checks my mouthguard and gloves before letting me in. I roam around the outside. Not to pump up the crowd, although it also seems to serve that purpose, but to re-familiarize myself with the size and feel of the ring.

When Ricky's song comes over the speakers, I return to my place and wait for him to arrive. He's a big guy—bigger than me—and he moves with the kind of swagger that lets you know he's used to being the alpha in every room he enters. But if he believes I'll submit to him, he's got another think coming. He leaps into the cage and circles the interior. The umpire calls us to the center and outlines the rules. We bump gloves, back off, and the timer starts.

Ricky comes forward hard, just as I expected him to. Pivoting to the side, I dodge out of his way and slam my shin across his stomach. First point of the match goes to me.

Damn right.

The fight continues in the same vein. He attacks, I evade and counter. He's getting frustrated; I can tell by the way his nostrils flare and his face flushes. But there isn't much he can do about it because I'm used to guys like him who think they can bash their way out of any situation, and I thrive on knocking them down blow by blow. A few of his shots land, but not enough to do any real damage, and finally, three rounds in, he reaches the point where his desperation to win overcomes his good sense. He charges forward, retribution in his eyes, and with a quick, easy movement I sweep him to the ground, then wrestle him into a choke hold. The ground isn't my favorite place to be, but Jase's ground game rocks, and a little of that rubs off on me. Enough that Ricky DeSilva submits.

Everything passes quickly after that. I'm clapped on the back and congratulated. Before long, Seth puts himself between me and the screaming audience, allowing me to leave the cage. I hurry out back, where I whiz through the shower and dress in my tux. Then I'm on the way to the wedding.

Sydney

I zip up the royal blue dress, which is tight across my bust—but not overly so—and check myself out in the mirror. "What do you think?"

Lena sticks two fingers between her lips and wolf-whistles. "You look hot. Gabe is a dipshit for not gluing himself to your side." She and I are nearly matching, our dresses slightly different shades.

"That's what I like to hear. You don't think it's too much?" There's a whole lot of cleavage on display.

"Hell, no. You always downplay yourself, but it's about time you showed the world how gorgeous you are."

Most of the time I don't have the chance to show off my figure or fashion sense. Scrubs don't do anyone any favors.

"Mom wants me to wear black."

Lena shrugs. "Black, blue, close enough." She runs a hand over her hair, which is knotted on the back of her head, checking for stray strands, then she leans over my shoulder and refreshes her lipstick. It's red, as per usual, and she rocks it. "Who wears black to a wedding anyway? Isn't that more funereal?"

This draws a laugh from me. "Maybe that's what tonight is—for the groom. You haven't met my family yet. I'll have to thank Jase for letting me borrow you. Did you tell him what we were doing tonight?"

She shakes her head. "Didn't think you'd appreciate me telling him because of the whole Gabe-ditching-you thing." Her upper lip curls into a sneer. "And to think, he used to be my favorite."

"Who, Gabe?" I sigh. "Don't hold it against him for my sake. I've always ranked lower in his priorities than fighting and I shouldn't have expected that to change. At least, not all at once."

"Well, he shouldn't have tripped at the first hurdle, either. Did you tell him how much this meant to you?"

I squirm. "Kind of. I mean, we didn't have a heart-to-heart but I told him it was a big deal, and I'm sure he knew how much this would bother me."

"Yeah, but he's a guy. They're not exactly known for being intuitive."

"Wouldn't it be nice if they were?" I muse.

"Hell, yeah."

I accessorize with elegant heels and silver jewelry, then check my makeup, satisfied that none of my family members will have grounds to accuse me of not dressing nicely enough. Lena wears a form-fitting dress, which makes her porcelain skin look flawless.

I hook my arm through hers. "I'm going to have the hottest date there. All my male cousins will be so jealous."

She rolls her eyes. "You don't have to butter me up. I'm already coming."

"I know." I squeeze her hand. "Just don't change your mind once we get there."

My family can be overwhelming, to say the least, and I don't mean that in a good way. We drive to the venue in Lena's Nissan, because I don't own a car, having no reason to need one regularly. The wedding is at an upmarket hotel—not because my family is wealthy, but because they're pretentious—and she pulls up and hands her keys to a valet. Together, we make our way inside.

"Thanks for being amazing," I say, once again. "I'm not sure I'd be able to endure this without you."

"You're very welcome, Syd. But once I get my hands on your boyfriend, he's going to regret choosing the fight over this."

Sighing, I say, "I wish you wouldn't."

To be honest, I should have just come right out and asked him to choose me over the fight, but I didn't have the emotional capacity to risk rejection when I was ninety percent sure he'd already decided to say yes and I was exhausted from a long shift.

By design, we arrive only minutes before the ceremony and duck into the back row. The audience are a sea of black and gray, with only a couple of splashes of color. I spy my parents near the front, and Mom gives me a stern look over her shoulder that implies I should have been earlier. As per usual, her inky black hair is bound in an elegant knot and her makeup perfectly complements her skin, which is a shade darker than my own. Her gaze lands on Lena, and one brow jumps up, then she cocks her head. I shake mine, not prepared to hold a silent conversation across a room, and she turns her back.

"Your mom?" Lena guesses.

"That's her, all right. Can you sense all the motherly vibes she's giving off?"

Lena snort-laughs, then flushes red, clapping a hand over her mouth. "You don't get along with her?"

I instantly feel disloyal. The woman gave birth to me, after all, but I'm pretty sure I was a mistake, and ever since then I've managed to remain a disappointment.

"I think you've got that the wrong way around. I might not mind her if she were more interested in me, but she's made it plain she doesn't agree with my priorities and that I'm constantly letting her down. That's when she remembers that I exist at all, which is usually only when we have to attend something like this."

"Ouch." She winces. "Sorry, babe."

"No worries. I'm over it." Or at least, I like to pretend I am.

The ceremony flows without a hitch. Christina is a beautiful bride, doing the Coleman name proud— something I'll no doubt hear later. As soon as it's done, we follow the wedding party into the restaurant where dinner is being served. They took photographs earlier in the day, and the cake cutting will happen after speeches are given.

Unfortunately, dinner does not go as well as the ceremony. For starters, we're seated at a table with my parents, and the moment my butt touches the chair, Mom is leaning over to hiss in my ear, "Where is Gabriel? You told me you'd have a date."

Wishing I could melt into the seat and disappear, I reach for a glass of wine and take a deep gulp. "Something urgent came up, so he couldn't join me. This is my friend Lena."

"Hello, Mrs. Coleman." Lena offers a hand, which Mom accepts, making a show of checking her other one for a ring. Seeing it bare, she looks at me with disdain. I know exactly what she's thinking. Mom believes half the reason I'm single is because I surround myself with other single women, AKA the competition. She honestly doesn't realize how outdated that view is.

"Lovely to meet you," she says, dismissing Lena before she's even released her hand. For a moment, I'm tempted to mention who Lena's parents are, just to see the look on her face—the LaFontaines are at the top of the societal ladder, exactly where Mom wishes she was —but I won't subject Lena to that.

"Hey, kid," Dad says, leaning around her and giving me the first genuine smile I've received from a family member all evening. His face is flushed pink and sweat beads on his receding hairline. I summon the best smile I can. My father has a decent heart; it's just unfortunate that he doesn't seem to think of me unless I'm right in front of him.

"Hi, Dad," I reply. "Good to see you."

My mother harrumphs. "I can't believe you didn't wear black. It's the most classic and flattering shade."

"Mom, it's a wedding. Can you not see what's wrong with that image? It's supposed to be a celebration."

She shakes her head. "Forgive me if it doesn't feel like a celebration so much as yet another reminder of how my only daughter still hasn't managed to attract and keep a good man." Her gaze rakes over me critically. "That dress doesn't do anything for you. Have you learned nothing from your cousins' sense of style?"

"You don't think she looks nice?" Lena cuts in, eyes flashing dangerously. She's a hothead, but at this moment, I love her for it. "She's absolutely gorgeous, and if you paid attention, you'd notice that a lot of the men here agree with me."

They do? I glance around but don't see anyone

looking this way. Mom makes a sound of disbelief but drops the topic when Dad mutters something under his breath. We sit through dinner, which is both classy and delicious, and listen to far too many long speeches that I'm secretly grateful for because they save me from conversing with my parents. Finally, the formal part of the evening ends and we're escorted to a ballroom, where a live band is set up.

"This is more like it," I murmur to Lena. There's a bar against one wall and I beeline toward it while the happy couple have their first dance. Lena follows, and we each grab a glass of champagne and clink them in a silent toast. Then the song changes and Lena takes my glass, sets it aside, and drags me onto the floor.

"I wasn't done with that," I protest.

"Don't care." She turns to face me and shimmies her hips. Many positive things can be said about Lena, but she is not a stellar dancer. "You've been moping all evening and you need to let loose and have a good time. Screw Gabe."

"That's exactly what I'd like to be doing," I call back, and she laughs and swats my arm.

I mimic her movements, but my heart isn't in it. She's right, I've been down ever since I realized Gabe planned to desert me, and even though she's being an incredible friend—probably better than I deserve at the moment—I can't stop thinking about where I stand in Gabe's priorities. That is, clearly *not* at the top of the list.

"Stop pouting," she says, swaying closer. "Try to have fun." She grabs my hands and we swing our arms, veering into each other and pulling away again in time with the beat. Leaning closer, she raises her voice to be heard above the noise. "Don't deny yourself just because your boyfriend is being an ass, and your mom is a piece of work. Your needs are important too, and right now, you need to stop thinking."

She's right, again, because of course she is. She's great at reading others because she ferrets out people's secrets and then protects them for a living. She also happens to understand the perils of dating an MMA fighter and having emotionally distant parents. Except our situations aren't the same because Jase is completely and undeniably devoted to her. I can't say that when it comes to Gabe. Shoving the thought to the back of my mind, I straighten my spine and make an effort to smile.

"Sorry. Officially forgetting them."

"Good girl."

We dance together for another few minutes, and then someone taps me on the shoulder. Twisting around, I see a hot guy in a suit, the top few buttons of his shirt undone and a sheen of perspiration on his forehead. He grins, his baby blues twinkling down at me, and offers me a hand.

I start to shake my head. "Oh, no. I—"

"Go!" Lena hisses, shoving my shoulder. "Have fun. Just don't do anything too crazy."

"I don't know..." I hedge.

She puts her mouth beside my ear. "Gabe blew it tonight. He deserves to know you danced with another man. Just don't let any hands or mouths wander to inappropriate places."

Still not entirely comfortable, but pleased by the idea of making Gabe jealous, I accept the guy's hand and let him pull me away.

18

By the time I make it to the hotel where the wedding is being held, it's dark outside and the night is growing late. The ceremony will be long over. The dinner, too, most likely, but I need to see Sydney and let her know that I remember her, and I care. I'm tired, but I need to prove I made the right choice in taking the fight, and I won't be certain until I see her smile and tell me it's okay.

At the reception desk, I ask for directions, relieved once again that the fight was so one-sided because I don't have any facial bruises or wounds that will freak anyone out. When I reach the ballroom where the band is playing, I pause in the doorway. Scanning the guests, I search for Sydney, but what I see is infinitely more frightening. Lena is striding toward me, chin raised, nostrils flared, and murder in her eyes.

Oh, shit.

Normally, I get on just fine with Jase's girl, but something tells me I'm not going to like what she's got to say.

"Hey, Lena."

"Nuh-uh," she snaps, holding up a hand. "Stop right there. Sydney does *not* need to see you tonight." She waves her hands, ushering me out. When the door closes, separating us from the wedding guests, she turns on me. "You absolute ass. How dare you show up here?"

"I, uh..." Her reaction has caught me off guard, and I don't know how to handle it. "I thought it'd be nice to surprise Sydney."

She shakes her head. "'Nice' would've been not ditching her in the first place. You turning up here isn't about her. It's about you making yourself feel better. But guess what, Gabe? You hurt her, and nothing can change that. You chose an MMA fight—one that wasn't even a big deal—over her, and you know where that tells her she ranks in your priorities?"

"That's not how it is," I protest, knowing it sounds weak. "She said I should take the fight, and I even arranged for it to happen earlier, so I could make it here."

"Not good enough." She jabs me in the chest with each word, not even mildly afraid of me despite the fact I'm twice her size and sporting a glare. "Some things matter more than MMA, and if you can't see that, then you don't deserve her."

The disappointed line of her mouth and the fire flashing in her eyes tell me there's no point in arguing with her tonight, but nor do I want Sydney to think I completely abandoned her, or that I don't care. I fucking hate the thought of hurting her and not being able to do a damn thing about it.

"I need to see Syd."

To my surprise, she relents, leading me back inside, but she stops me before we've taken two steps into the ballroom and points out my beautiful girl, who's

157

dancing with a blond man and wearing a hesitant smile. She's dancing *with another man*.

My heart automatically rebels. Not okay.

"It took me hours to get her to relax like that," Lena murmurs. "She's finally enjoying herself, no thanks to you, so think carefully about whether you're prepared to ruin that."

Okay, she's successfully made me feel like a terrible person. Watching Sydney, I look for signs of strain on her face, and find them. Her eyes are tinged with red, and even though she's smiling, it doesn't meet her eyes. My stomach bottoms out, leaving me feeling hollow and empty. Lena is right. I upset her, even if I didn't mean to, but I can't stand here and let someone else make it better, either. I need to try.

Pushing past Lena, I stride over to Sydney and her companion.

"Gabe!" Her eyes widen, and her cheeks are flushed. With joy? Because she's had too much to drink? Or something else? "What are you doing here?"

"I told you I'd come as soon as I could." I kiss her lips, although she seems too shocked to respond, then jerk my head at the guy. "Thanks for looking after her, but she's with me now."

Her jaw drops. "Excuse me?" The words are a squeak. Barely audible.

The guy's gaze flickers to her, a question in it. He looks vaguely familiar but I can't put my finger on where I know him from.

"You can't just barge in here and... and..." she sputters.

"Yeah?" I prompt, not sure where she's going with this.

"And take over like you didn't ditch me!" Her voice

rises, and people are starting to stare. Yeah, she's definitely had a few drinks.

My shoulders hunch, but they don't deflect the attention. "I just wanna dance."

She pouts. "Well, you don't get to dance with me tonight. And you definitely don't get to send away my dance partner just because you don't approve. You chose not to be here."

"But now I am." I gesture around to show that I am, indeed, here.

"Syd, is everything okay?" the guy asks.

"Yeah, we're fine, Shaun," she says. "Thanks for double-checking, but it's all right if you want to go now. I'm not dancing with him." She points at me. "But I'm not worried about him, either."

Shaun doesn't move. "I don't think she wants you here."

His attitude is starting to annoy me. "And I don't think you get an opinion. Who are you again?"

"Sydney's cousin." He folds his arms over his chest. "On her father's side. We're in town for the wedding. Who the hell are you?"

Her cousin. *Fuck*. Not what I expected.

"I'm, uh..." I risk a glance at her and find her glaring. "Her boyfriend."

They exchange a look, and a tingle runs down my spine. I don't like the sense I'm getting from Sydney. A hand lands on my arm. It's Lena.

"I think you should do what she says."

I want to argue, but I can see that Sydney isn't in a good frame of mind for a proper conversation, and I deflate. It'll have to wait until the morning.

"Okay." I bend to kiss her cheek, but she turns her face away. "I'll call in the morning, *cariño*."

Reluctantly, I turn and leave.

Sydney

Ugh. I roll over in bed, my stomach roiling. It's been so long since I was hungover that my body doesn't know how to deal with it. Searching my memories, I try to recall what happened last night. I have flashes of the wedding ceremony, and of an uncomfortable dinner with my parents, then it's just throbbing music until... wait... Did Gabe turn up? I vaguely recall seeing his face. Too handsome. My heart hurting. Me giving him a piece of my mind. Groaning, I curl into a ball. A nerve in the back of my eye twitches, and my head is pounding like nobody's business.

Then the whole lot rushes back, along with a sense of loneliness that's overpowering. Gabe chose a fight instead of something he'd agreed to do with me. A fight that doesn't even mean anything in the grand scheme of things. And then he turned up only to try and jump right in as if it didn't matter, but it feels like there's a hole in my chest where my heart used to be.

How could he do that? He knows me better than anyone, which means he was aware of how I'd feel and did it anyway. The hollowness inside me turns into a yawning void, sucking any remaining positivity out of me.

I need ice cream. Even if I can't keep it down.

Traipsing to the kitchen, I make the mistake of switching on the lights and throw a hand up to shield my eyes until I can get them off again. In the dimly lit room, I rummage in the cupboard for painkillers and down them with a glass of water. The cold water hits my angry stomach the wrong way and I lunge for the sink, relieved when I don't throw up.

Why did I do this to myself? I haven't been more than tipsy in years. Resting my forehead on the cool countertop, I have to admit that it's all because I was stupid enough to believe Gabe could prioritize anything over MMA. He's been obsessed with living up to everyone's expectations since his very first fight, which got a lot of attention because he was following in his father's footsteps.

Since then, it's only gotten worse. With each win, the public debates whether he will eventually outdo his famous father, or if he'll fall short. They analyze his technique and his record and compare it to his father's at a similar age. Tomas is the worst of all. He means well, but he urges Gabe to do more, better, and faster, not seeing the impact it has on him.

I can understand why the pressure gets to Gabe, and why he doesn't want to disappoint anyone. It must be difficult. But even though I understand, I also know that when I settle down with someone, I want to be his obsession, and with Gabe, I struggle to believe that's a possibility. His career might always come first.

Do I resent that? Yeah, maybe a little, but I can't be mad with him either because my career is also important to me. I see where he's coming from. It just sucks. I straighten and go to the mini freezer, where I withdraw a small tub of Ben & Jerry's cookie dough ice cream. A minute later, I'm in bed, eating the ice cream straight from the tub. When I'm halfway through, my phone pings. I check the messages. It's from Gabe.

Gabe: *Morning, baby. How are you feeling? Want to do something later?*

As if I feel up to anything.

Sydney: *No thanks. Holed up in bed with ice cream. Feeling sorry for myself.*

Even if I were feeling well, I don't know that I'd want to see him. The cavalier way he treated his commitment to me this weekend doesn't bode well. If it were a one-off, I'd let it slide, but he was also late to dancing after *he* suggested it and then he was late to dinner earlier this week. Each incident on its own isn't a big deal, but combined with the times he's stood me up in the past? It's alarming.

The phone rings. I don't have to check to know it's him, and much as I might want to ignore him, that would only result in him driving over here. I may as well address this head-on.

"Hi, Gabe." I sound weary, even to my own ears.

"Syd." His husky voice wakes up my body in ways I wish it didn't. "What's wrong?"

Where to start? I jam the spoon into my ice cream and set it aside.

"You mean except for being hungover?" I groan. "I forgot how shitty this feels."

He chuckles but doesn't say anything, letting me continue at my own pace.

"I have a question for you."

"Shoot."

I pause, wetting my lips, unsure of whether I really want to know the answer. "If you have to make a similar choice in future—something with me versus a last-minute MMA event—would you choose differently?"

A silence hangs in the air between us.

Oh.

Oh.

"Sydney..." He sounds tormented, and maybe it makes me a bad person, but it's satisfying as hell. "I didn't choose MMA over you, and this was a one-off. The same situation isn't going to come up again."

"But if it did."

He ignores me. "Can I come over? I need to be with you."

"No." I hold up a hand as if he's standing in front of me. "Nuh-uh. I need the distance to think clearly."

"And what are you thinking?" His tone is soft. Wary.

"I'm thinking that I asked too much of you when we got together." I sigh. "You can't put me first. You don't know how to put anything ahead of MMA—including your own health—and I understand why, but my initial reason for looking for love elsewhere still stands. We want different things. I'm ready to commit the time and energy needed to build a relationship, and I just don't think you're there yet. I'm not saying that to be negative or to make you feel guilty, it's just the way it is. With where we each are in our lives, I don't think our relationship can work."

"Wait, what?" He sounds panicked. "Syd, it was one night, and you're ready to throw everything we have away? I'll make it up to you, *cariño*, I promise. As soon as the Ruby Knuckles is over, you and I can take a long weekend trip to the beach. I'll slow down for a while and spend some time with you. I know how much you've always wanted to go there."

His offer is tempting. So tempting. But I want more than whatever scraps of time he has left over between fight camps. I want to be part of his life all the time, not just when he can make room for me. No other fighter I've met trains as hard as him, and I respect his work ethic, but the fact remains that he could ease back his training by a fraction and carve out enough time to make me happy. He simply won't.

163

"No, Gabe. Spending time with me shouldn't be a chore, or another responsibility that you need to fulfill at a later date. I don't want to be a burden or something that brings you down. I want to be the thing you look forward to, and the person you turn down other things for because you can't stand being away from me."

"It's not like that," he protests. "Is this because of the fight? Can I remind you that you said I should do it?"

"After asking you to come to the wedding and getting told it was only one night. No big deal, right? Well, you know what? A fight is only one night too, and I've never belittled one of yours or made it seem unimportant. I've been there to support you every step of the way."

"I know you have. And I want to give you what you need."

"But you can't, can you?" I ask softly.

His silence speaks volumes, but after counting to five with no reply, I hear him say, "I'd like to try."

"I'm not sure if I'm brave enough to let you," I choke out.

"Please..."

"I need some space." I end the call.

19

GABE

I fucked up. I fucked up bad.

Worse, I didn't even realize how much I'd fucked up until now. Even if it bolstered my confidence, taking that fight wasn't worth losing Sydney. But then, I never believed I'd actually lose her, so how did I end up here? I was sure she'd look at me with disappointment—which would have been bad enough—and then give me the opportunity to redeem myself. By nature, she's a forgiving person. She doesn't hand out ultimatums or walk out on people after they screw up once.

Okay, so maybe it was more than once.

I don't know what to do, or how to handle this. I want to ride my motorcycle over to her place and bash on the door until she lets me in, then grovel until she admits she loves me, but something tells me that isn't the right tactic to take. She isn't reacting to things the way I'm accustomed to. She's making changes in her life, and I'm afraid that if I make one more misstep, cutting me out will be another of those changes. I can't let that happen. Not when I love her the way I do. And maybe I've been shitty at showing it, but I can do better.

Fuck.

I can't go over there in my current state. I'll say the wrong thing, or do the wrong thing, and then there'll be no recovering from it. But I can't do anything else, either. I won't be able to focus on training when I can hardly breathe and it feels like a hand is squeezing my heart. In fact, the only thing that might help me right now is liquor. A whole lot of it. Fight camp be damned.

Going to the cabinet, I find a bottle of gin and open it.

Half a dozen gin and tonics—heavy on the gin—later, I fall asleep.

Bzzt. My phone vibrates, and I swear it sounds angry. I ignore it. It's probably Jase or Devon. I've had five messages from each of them since I failed to turn up to training this morning. They're probably taking turns to contact me. I don't give a shit. I'm huddled in bed with my phone, scrolling through photos of Sydney and me.

There she is, wearing her graduation robe, eyes bright, my arm around her. God, the way we're leaning into each other makes it so obvious that we both wanted more, but neither of us were brave enough to take a risk. How long did we deprive ourselves of love by being too blind and scared to do anything about it?

And there she is after my first fight. My cheek is swollen, nose bleeding, and I'm covered in sweat, but she didn't let that stop her from hugging me like I'd won a title bout. Scrolling some more, I find a photo of her at our junior prom. We didn't go together because I was going through a selfish-bastard phase and blew her off every time a pretty girl batted her eyelashes, but she stuck with me anyway. She was beautiful that day, in a pastel pink dress, arm in arm with my friend Max—the only guy I trusted not to get handsy with her. Back then I may not have viewed her as a woman, but other boys at school sure as hell did, and they all knew if they messed with her, I'd break their faces. For that night, Max treated her like a goddamned princess. The way I should be treating her now that we're together.

"Fuck," I mutter, feeling like a piece of shit.

Someone thumps on the door, and I ignore them, huddling deeper into the blankets. At least one good thing has come of this: I've caught up on my rest.

A key slides into the lock and footsteps pound down the hall toward my bedroom. The door flies open and I shield my eyes from the sudden light.

"What the hell?" Through the glare, I can make out Jase and Devon. "Fuck off, assholes."

"Bro, what is going on with you?" Jase demands, striding to the curtains and tearing them open. "We haven't seen or heard from you since Saturday. You've been ignoring our texts, Seth is spitting fucking nails, and your dad is going to have an aneurism. He says he's called and come by and you haven't answered the phone or the door. You're lucky he didn't break in. Valentina told him to be patient." His eyes go to the gin on the dresser, and his jaw tenses. "Have you been drinking?"

"Yeah," I admit, because he can probably smell it in the air anyway. I haven't drunk myself stupid, but a few G&Ts go a long way when you haven't touched the stuff in ages.

"Seth is gonna kick your ass," Devon says a little too

gleefully. "If Tomas doesn't do it first." Seeing the phone on the bed, he snatches it up and smiles when he spots the photo of Sydney, Max, my date, and me at junior prom. "Wow, would you look at this?" He thrusts the phone at Jase. "Gabe had a baby mustache. Don't know how you hooked the girls with that caterpillar on your lip."

But as Devon chuckles to himself, Jase's gaze flicks to the photograph and then sharpens. "Something happened with Sydney?" he asks, seeing through me in an instant.

I guess it's easy to recognize woman-induced moping when you've been through the same thing your-self. Not that Jase ever wallowed in his bed. He directed his energy into winning his next fight. Unfortunately for me, my next fight is a good part of the problem. If not for that, and the responsibility I have to my father, I wouldn't have done anything to make Sydney feel like I don't care.

Sitting up, I reach for the glass of water on the cabinet beside my bed and take a gulp, moistening my dry throat. "I think we might be on a break. I'm a little foggy on exactly where we stand."

"Oh, hell," Devon exclaims, slapping me on the back. "I'm sorry, man. What happened?"

"The wedding," Jase says, understanding dawning on his face.

Wincing, I ask, "You knew?"

He shrugs. "Lena said she was doing something with Sydney on Saturday. Didn't tell me ahead of time, but she might have mentioned it when she got home that night."

"Wait." Devon's eyes widen. "Syd dumped you

because you couldn't go to some wedding with her? That's rough."

"It's not just that," I admit. "I've been late or missed so many things because of training that I think she reached a hard limit." Slowly, I lever myself out of bed. I'm wearing boxers, so they don't see anything they haven't before. To Jase, I add, "Your girl just about tore me a new one on Saturday. Gave me this massive guilt trip." One I still haven't recovered from.

Devon makes himself at home on my bed. "Did you deserve it?"

"Yeah. Maybe."

"That doesn't matter right now, Dev," Jase says, then turns to me. "You gotta pull yourself together. If Seth finds out you've been sulking like a teenaged girl, it's not going to be good for you. As it is, he's furious. You need to shower, because honestly, you stink, and then you need to get dressed. We're going to the gym, and you're going to go through the motions and make Seth—and your dad—happy. Or at least not want to strangle you. Got it?"

I shake my head, and the room spins. Lurching, I grab onto the dresser to stabilize myself. Fuck, when was the last time I ate? I don't even remember. I might have had something yesterday morning. But my stomach isn't the only thing that feels hollow. There's a space inside my heart that used to be occupied by Sydney Coleman— my best friend and the most beautiful woman in the entire goddamned world. The emptiness sucks at me like a vacuum, trying to swallow everything else around it.

"What's the point?" I ask bleakly. "Nothing matters without her."

Jase's brows pinch together, and I can tell his

patience is drawing to an end, but I can't find it in me to care.

"Pull yourself together." This comes from Devon. "You're not going to win her back like this."

"What if I can't win her back at all?"

Something whacks me across the back of the head. It's Jase, and when I whirl around, I can see his temper has finally snapped. "You're being pathetic. If you truly feel that strongly about her, then do something about it. Don't give up that easily."

My shoulders slump. "She doesn't know if she can trust me. What am I supposed to do with that?" If she's done with me, I respect her decision, even if it's killing me inside.

"You've got to fight for her," he urges. "Show her what she's worth to you."

This time, I hear him. All Sydney has been asking for is a person who knows her worth and treats her like she's precious. Maybe Jase and Devon are right. Maybe it's not too late for me to prove to her that I can be that person.

"I'll think on it," I reply, nodding slowly. "Thanks for coming to get me."

"Always," Devon says. "Bring it in, guys."

I protest as he and Jase descend on me in a three-way hug that pushes all my boundaries, but I just stand there and take it because these assholes are the closest thing I have to brothers, and I love them. Even if they drive me crazy sometimes.

Devon pulls back, his nose wrinkling. "Seriously, bro. Wash yourself. You need it."

Yeah. Brotherly love. Rolling my eyes, I let the comment go and head for the bathroom. "Be out soon."

20

SYDNEY

The Friday after the wedding—which, incidentally, is ten missed calls and twenty-seven unanswered texts later—I head to Jase's place to visit Lena, who has more or less moved in with him. She still has her apartment, but I doubt she will for much longer. There's no point in her paying rent when she's at his enormous house every night anyway.

"Oh, honey," she says when she opens the door, and then scoops me into a hug. "Has it been a tough week?"

"Only a lot." Trying not to sniffle on her shoulder, I return her hug, squeezing tightly. I hope Jase knows how lucky he is to have Lena, because she's incredible. She leads me inside, heading for the living room, where we plan to snuggle up and watch a movie.

"Tell me about it," she prompts.

I shrug, not wanting to rehash my crappy week. "Gabe was Gabe. Mom sent me a diet plan and Cosmo's top ten tips for meeting eligible men."

"Ugh." She pulls a face. "Rough. But you know, your

mom might be onto something. Maybe we should reactivate your dating account."

The words fall flat between us. I know she means well, but I'm not ready yet. Maybe in another few weeks. Or maybe Gabe Mendoza will always own a corner of my heart.

"Not this time," I tell her. "I hope you found the scariest thriller you could. I'm in the mood for screaming."

She laughs. "You're in luck. I've got the latest Netflix slasher film lined up. I've heard terrible things."

"What did I do to deserve you?" Flopping onto an oversized sofa, I wait while she heads to the kitchen. She returns a moment later holding two mugs, with a bag of potato chips tucked under her arm. She hands me one of the mugs, and I sniff its contents, then raise an eyebrow in surprise. "This is wine."

"So it is." She grins. "Figured a mug might be harder to spill than a glass. Plus it fits more."

I raise it in a mock toast. "You thought of everything."

She settles beside me and clinks my mug, then reaches over to start the movie.

We're half an hour in when I hear cars in the driveway, and freeze.

"Are we expecting anyone?"

Cursing, Lena checks the time. "It's probably the boys. They'd planned to watch some of Gabe's opponent's fights to prep, but Jase said they wouldn't be here until later."

Oh crap. Just what I don't need. I can't bear the thought of seeing Gabe's stupidly gorgeous face when I've been successfully avoiding him. I haven't even read any of his texts because I'm afraid I won't be strong enough to stand my ground.

"Do you want to hide in one of the other rooms?" Lena asks, eyes wide, as the sound of footfalls and voices draws nearer.

"No." Straightening my shoulders, I set my mug of wine aside and brace for the inevitable. "I can do this."

I won't run. I'm a part of this group of friends, and whether he brought me into the fold or not, I don't intend to lose them just because Gabe and I are uncomfortable around each other. A moment later, they come into view. Jase spots us first and stops short, swearing. Devon nearly runs into the back of him, and Gabe steps to the side to avoid them. Unfortunately, this gives him a clear line of sight to me.

He freezes, and I can instantly see that he hasn't been doing any better than I have. His eyes are bloodshot, his jaw is scruffy and unshaven, and he's recently cut his hair, which is cropped close to his skull.

"Syd," he breathes.

"Oh, fuck," Devon groans, grabbing his arm and trying to tug him away, but Gabe is bigger and doesn't budge. My heart lurches at the sight of him, and he looks so tortured that I ache to run my hand over his stubbly jaw and assure him everything will be okay. But everything isn't okay, and I can't mess with his head like that when I know things aren't right between us, so I stay where I am and pretend I'm glued to the sofa.

"Bro, come on," Jase says, shoving his arm. "Let's go watch those videos."

"Not yet," he replies, taking a step toward me. "Sydney, baby, can we talk in private?"

Pressing my lips together, I shake my head. If he gets me alone, all of my resolve will sail out the window.

"Okay, then." He cracks his neck from side to side and sucks in air. "I'll say this in front of everyone."

Uh-oh. I have a sinking feeling I may have made the wrong decision. Heat crawls up my cheeks. What does he think he's doing?

He drops to his knees, and behind him, Devon claps a hand over his eyes. I want to do the same. Whatever he's about to say, I just know it's going to make things ten times harder.

"I love you, Sydney. I'm hooked on you. My heart is all yours, and I'm not giving up on you. I'll even pull out of my big fight if you want, but I'm not letting you go without making sure you know exactly how much you mean to me." His expression is gut-wrenchingly sincere, and I can't believe he's doing this. He's splaying himself out in front of everyone. Making himself vulnerable. But that doesn't change the fact that all he's giving me are words. I need to see actions to back those up, so I can believe in our future.

"Gabe, no. Don't do this," I plead. "Not right now. Give it time, and we can talk about things. But you need your head to be in the ring, and I need space. I told you that."

His gaze drops from mine to the floor, becoming blank, and I hate it. I *hate* that I'm doing this to him. But I need to look out for me, and he needs to respect my boundaries.

"I'm not giving up on you." His voice is quiet but strong, and it rolls over me like velvet. "I'll prove how much I care."

And then he stands and allows his friends to guide him away.

"You're fucking crazy," I hear Devon tell him as they pass into another room.

I shake my head, hardly able to believe what just happened.

"That was intense," Lena murmurs.

"Yeah." I grab my purse and stand. "I'm going to go."

She leaps to her feet. "Don't let him chase you out. I'll make sure Jase keeps him away."

"No, it's okay. I'm just shaken up. I need to be on my own."

I head for the door and she joins me. "Call if you need to, okay? I'm here for you whenever."

"Thanks, Lee." I kiss her cheek. "Wish him luck for me, if I don't see him before the fight."

"I will."

A while later, I'm home, but it takes many more hours before my nerves settle enough to have any peace.

Gabe

A little over a week later, the day of my fight against Leo Delaney arrives, and I have a decision to make. Ever since I saw Sydney at Jase's place last Friday, I've been trying to get in touch with her. Calling, texting, knocking on her door—although God knows if she was there or not because I don't have a copy of her schedule. Hell, I even sent an email, and all I've received in response is crickets.

Today, I'm not letting her brush me off or avoid me. I'm not afraid of hard work, and I have plenty of patience—just ask anyone at the gym. I'm going to use those qualities to take the next step with Sydney. I want her in my life. In order to be whole, I *need* her, and I've never gone down without a fight so there's no reason to start now. But first, it's time I have a heart to heart with my father.

I eat a big breakfast, then organize my gear bag for the evening, double checking that my mouthguard and groin cup are accounted for. I shower, change into comfortable track pants, a sleeveless shirt, and a hoodie, then pack enough sandwiches and snacks to feed an army. Finally, I strap the bag onto my motorcycle and ride it to Mama and Dad's place. I already know Mama is away because I bought a salon voucher for her and one of her friends. I'm also reasonably sure Dad will be there, reviewing past fights and searching for any last-minute advice he can share with me. That's how he is. He supports me, and he wants the best for me. And that's why, even though this is going to be hard, I know that, in the end, he'll understand.

I park beside the house, head up to the house, and knock. A few moments later, he opens the door.

"Hi, *Papa*."

"Gabe." His brow furrows. "What are you doing here? You should be at home resting."

I loosen my jaw, which has tightened in anticipation of the upcoming conversation. "There's something we've got to talk about."

"Oh?" He stands aside and lets me in. Sure enough, in the living room there's an image of me frozen on the TV screen. He sits, and gestures for me to do the same. I'm full of restless energy and would rather pace, but I know it will make him more comfortable so I join him.

"Sydney and I had a falling out over the DeSilva fight."

"I noticed she wasn't there."

I nod. "Her cousin was getting married. I'd said I'd be there."

176

"Ah." He winces. "Women don't take it well when you let them down."

"I know." I swallow, terrified of what I'm about to say even though I know beyond a shadow of a doubt that it's the right thing to do. "She hasn't been talking to me, and now I've got to do something and I'm afraid I'll disappoint *you*."

His expression flickers, and I think he sees what's coming.

"I need Sydney to know she means more to me than any fight, and in order to prove that, it might mean missing the event tonight."

An invisible shadow descends on him. "Why tonight? Why can't it be another fight? We've worked so hard for this, *mijo*. It's your dream."

"No," I say gently. "It's yours. Don't get me wrong, I'd love to be the Ruby Knuckles champion—it'd be an honor—but it's not my dream. I've been wrapped up in competing and proving myself and making you proud for so long that I lost sight of what really matters to me. It's her, and I'm not going to lose her."

Dad gapes, and there's sadness in his eyes. Shock, too. I wish I could erase it. Wish I'd figured out how the hell I felt before being forced into this position, but the situation sucks and I'm doing the best I can with it.

"But you love MMA," he argues. "You want to be the best."

"I do love it," I agree. "As far as careers go, it's the only one I want. I belong in a ring. But I need Sydney." Desperate for him to understand, I add, "Don't you need Mama like that? If you'd had to choose, wouldn't you have chosen her?"

Slowly, he nods. His skin is unusually pale, and he

mops a hand down his face, groaning. "What a goddamned mess."

"I'm sorry." I really am.

Rubbing his temples, he raises his gaze back to mine. "You're right. Valentina is my everything. There's nothing I wouldn't do for that woman." He pinches the bridge of his nose between his thumb and forefinger, and sighs. "I guess you'd better go get your girl."

I break into a grin. "Thanks, *Papa*."

I was going to do it regardless, but his approval, even if it's reluctant, means a lot.

"*Te quiero, mijo*. I love you, and you're my son first and foremost." He folds me into a hug and slaps me on the back. "Now, get the hell going."

As I make for the exit, he calls, "And *try* to be there. For me."

"I will, *Papa*. Bye."

It's a short trip to Sydney's apartment building. As I carry my bag upstairs and head for her apartment, nerves riot in my belly, and they have nothing to do with Dad or the Ruby Knuckles. Right now, Sydney matters more to me than whatever kudos, money, or approval I'll get for taking out Leo.

When I reach her door, I knock, praying she's home and not at work. There's no response, but after a few moments of straining my ears, I hear a faint rustle on the other side, as if she's peeking through the peephole.

"I know you're there," I say, with more confidence than I feel. "Please let me in." She doesn't respond, but a brief scuffle indicates I'm right. Knocking again, I call, "I owe you an apology, and we need to have a conversation."

Silence.

With a sigh, I sink to the floor, my back against the

door, and make myself comfortable. I'm not going to let myself in when she doesn't want me there because that's a surefire way to push her even further away. "If you're going to be that way then I suppose I'll just have to sit here all day and wait you out."

This time, I hear a scoff. "Will not. You have a fight to be at tonight."

"Don't care." Much as it's hard to believe, it's the truth. If it comes down to a choice between this one fight and keeping Sydney forever, I'll choose her every time. I understand why she doesn't believe me. My priorities have been messed up in the past, but now that my head is screwed on straight, I'm not going anywhere. "You'd better believe I'll stay right here until you're ready to talk, sweetheart. However long that takes. I have enough food here to keep me going for a good while."

"Please don't make a scene," she begs. "Just go. Do your thing. I can't handle seeing you right now." Her voice breaks on the last sentence, and my hands tighten into fists.

"No one is making a scene," I promise. "I'm just sitting here nice and quietly. You let me in when you're ready."

"Gabe." She sounds annoyed. "Please. Don't do this."

"I won't give up on us, sweetheart. Things are all kinds of wrong, and I want to fix it, which means I'll be staying here and boycotting my fight if that's what it takes to prove to you where you rank for me." I mean it, one hundred percent. I'm staging a sit-in, and I won't be moved.

She huffs, and in that soft breath I hear months' worth of bottled-up frustration—if not years. "If you're trying to guilt me into letting you in so you make it to your fight on time, don't bother. I won't let you manipu-late me."

"Good, because I don't want that." I can see why it would cross her mind though. After all, I left it until the day of the fight to put my foot down. But that's only because I have this awful feeling that if I go along tonight without resolving things between us, it will be too late. The damage to our relationship will be irrevocable. I can't let that happen.

"I'm not here to guilt you. I'm here to talk this through. To make it better."

For a long moment, she doesn't reply, and I think I hear her groan under her breath. The door handle turns, and my gaze shoots to it, my entire body tensing, ready to leap up the second it opens. But then she releases it, and the lock snicks back into place.

"Seriously, if you don't move I'll have to call the building manager," she says.

"If you feel like you need to, go ahead." Although I doubt the reedy guy I've seen bumming around in a polo shirt would dare to remove me from the premises. But if she really wants me gone that badly, I'll leave. Until then, I'll wait her out, because I don't truly believe that's what she wants. She's just trying to protect her heart. While it causes an ache in my own chest to know that she feels she needs to, I get it, and I intend to prove that I've finally grown up enough for her to trust me to keep it safe.

"Why are you so frustrating?" she asks, sounding so tired I wish I could gather her in my arms and hold her close.

"Because I can't think of any other way to prove myself to you, baby. When you're ready, I'll be here."

21

SYDNEY

Why did I have to fall in love with a guy who could out-stubborn a ram?

And exactly what is he planning to accomplish by camping outside my door?

All he's going to do is drive home exactly how much more MMA means to him than I do when he leaves. Either that, or he'll guilt me into letting him in, which means I'll only resent him more when he goes. All in all, it doesn't seem like the most well thought-out plan he could have devised. Plus, it's making me skittish. Moving around the apartment, I'm hyper conscious of every sound I make and can't help but wonder whether he can hear them, too, or if he can figure out what I'm doing based on the noises drifting through the door. The place isn't even remotely soundproof.

Still, I go about my day, doing the laundry and vacu-uming, watching an episode of a sitcom I love about a city girl who moves to the sticks, and then I've started making a grilled cheese sandwich for lunch when my phone rings. Grabbing it out of my pocket, I see the caller is Mrs. Ramirez, my neighbor from across the hall.

"Hey, Mrs. R. What's up?"

"Hello, Sydney dear," she rasps, her throat rough from cigarettes. "I just wanted to make sure you're okay. There's a man loitering in the hall by your door. He looks vaguely familiar but I can't quite place him. Is he causing you any trouble?"

I groan, dragging a hand down my face. Gabe is still out there? "No, he's fine. Don't you worry. Just a friend I'm having an argument with who can't stand losing."

"Oh." There's a pregnant pause, then she adds, "Are you sure? Because my nephew is a sergeant with the Metro PD. I can give him a call."

"No, no, no," I gasp, hoping she hasn't already contacted him. She's a lovely old lady but a tad interfering and it would be just like her to call her nephew with some exaggerated tale of a damsel in strife. "There's no need for that. I promise you, everything is fine. But thanks for checking in on me. How is Molly doing?" I ask, grasping at straws. Mrs. Ramirez is obsessed with her Maine Coon, Molly, and never misses an opportunity to talk about her.

She huffs. "You would not believe what happened yesterday." Ten minutes pass before she stops telling me about her cat. When the call ends, I'm tempted to reiterate to Gabe that he should leave, but I feel like ignoring him is probably the safest way to ensure he does. I smell something burning, and rush to save my grilled cheese. It's extra crispy, but edible. My stomach grumbles, and I think of Gabe outside. Should I make him a sandwich?

No, of course not!

But maybe he's hungry. He needs to be well-fueled for tonight.

It's not your problem. Besides, he said he has food.

Ugh. With immense willpower, I manage to squelch the need to take care of my friend and eat by myself. Then I climb into bed—because it's easily the most comfortable place in the apartment to read—and settle in with a romance novel.

Eventually, I glance at the clock and realize it's time to get ready and go to the stadium if I want to see Gabe's fight. Regardless of our personal situation, he is my best friend and I want to be there supporting him for the biggest match of his life. I dress in jeans, but then catch sight of myself in the mirror and can't help but think "Meh". I look bland and boring. It's the biggest night of Gabe's career and if I'm going to be at his side, I want to look my best. I swap the jeans for a slinky silver dress that hugs my curves. I take a few moments to do my makeup, adding a sweep of bright pink lipstick and some shimmer powder.

I smile at my reflection. Better.

I head to the door. When I open it, a large body sprawls inward. My stomach dips with disbelief, and a light fluttering begins in my chest. I rub a hand over it. He's *here*. Outside my apartment. When he should be preparing to face off against Leo Delaney. I'm struggling to get my head around the idea while he leaps to his feet with a catlike grace that belies his size, and gawks at me.

"You—uh—" He stutters. "You're fucking gorgeous." He reaches for me, but then his hand drops to his side. "You've never looked more beautiful."

My cheeks heat. "Thank you. I wanted to make an effort."

"I can tell." He looks unsure of himself. "Does this mean we can talk?"

My gaze skims down him, cataloging every detail, including the bag at his feet. "You should be at the stadium."

He shakes his head, his dark eyes never leaving my face. They search my features, and I feel like an insect under a magnifying glass. He's trying to see into my soul, and it leaves me on edge.

"I'm not going. You're more important."

With a sigh, I beg the universe for patience. "That's very sweet, but you're going to ruin your career. Not to mention your relationship with your dad."

He shrugs one massive shoulder and takes a step closer. "Dad and I are good. As for the event? It'll go on without me. I'm not moving."

Frustration surges within me. Every bit of annoyance that I've ever suppressed roars to the surface, and I march up to him and lay my hands on his chest, fully intending to shove him. But then something unusual happens. My fingers curl into the soft fabric of his sleeveless shirt and hold him there.

"You're being crazy," I growl as his enticing male scent wafts over me, leaving me light-headed. He shifts beneath my palms, and I can feel the firm muscles of his chest gliding as his hands go to my hips.

"No, Syd." His tone is firm, and there's no mistaking his body language. Staunch. Unmovable. "*You're* crazy if you think I'm ever going to rank a stupid fight above you again." His face tilts closer, his lips only a few inches above mine, which tingle with anticipation, yearning for me to get on with it and close the distance between us. Pressing my lips together doesn't help, but it draws his focus to my mouth, and he exhales sharply. "I want to kiss you so goddamn much."

"Please," I whisper, and I don't know if I'm begging him not to, or to go ahead and do it.

A shudder runs through him, and he closes his eyes. "I won't kiss you until I know whether we have a future. I couldn't stand getting a taste of you only to have you snatched away again. Let me in, baby. Let me fix this."

God, the way he's looking at me... Every place his stare lingers, I break out in goosebumps. I'd forgotten how addictive his touch is, and the attraction that explodes between us every time we're near. Now that we've held each other, stroked each other, and experienced overwhelming pleasure in each other's arms, the connection that's always simmered between us has become a blazing inferno and I'm almost powerless to resist.

Almost.

But I still have some control, and I exercise it now. "We can talk after your fight." Sucking in a breath, I hope I'm not making a mistake. "I'm coming with you."

GABE

Anticipation thrums in my veins as I let Sydney lead the way out of her apartment, staying close behind her. I'm not stupid enough to give her the opportunity to shut a door in my face. Whatever just passed between us, it felt like progress, but I don't want to get ahead of myself. Nerves and excitement jangle inside me and they have nothing to do with the fight—surprisingly, I'm not even pumped about that at all. No, this strange energy crawling over my skin is purely because of the beautiful woman in front of me. Her ass sways as she walks, and fuck, I want to grab it. I know how amazing those curves are in my hands, and that dress—*hell*, it's going to be the death of me, but I'll die happy. What does it mean that she's wearing it? Because my heart wants to believe that she glammed up to make me proud. Her choice of outfit gives me hope. Why would she bother looking her best if she didn't want me, deep down?

We get to my motorcycle and I secure my bag in place, then throw one leg over to sit astride it. Sydney slides on behind me, wrapping her arms around my middle, all of her softness pressing into my back. My dick stirs, and when I start the engine, she wriggles even closer, erasing any hint of air between our bodies. I stiffen. I'm eager for this fight to be over so I can finally say everything to her that I need to, and then love her the way she deserves—hard and deep and tender.

The motorcycle lurches forward, and then we're on our way, buildings blurring past us. Even though I drive carefully because her legs are exposed, it doesn't take nearly as long as I'd like before we arrive. There's something blissful about being on your bike with your girl wrapped around you. And yeah, maybe she's spitting mad, but she's still my girl, and she promised to hear me out, which buoys me as we park and approach the stadium. A bouncer stands at the rear entrance, and nods as we pass.

Inside, several people hurry toward me, but one glare sends them packing, and Sydney and I make our way—unhindered—down the corridor to the room that's been reserved for Crown MMA Gym. She doesn't say a word, but I notice several men checking her out, and I narrow my eyes at them and watch as they duck their heads and scurry away. Satisfaction blasts through me, along with a mantra that plays on repeat in my mind.

Get in, bust heads, claim my girl. Get in, bust heads, claim my girl.

"About fucking time," Jase snaps as I step into the changing room.

"Where the fuck have you been?" Seth demands, nostrils flaring, face dangerously red. His pale greenish eyes flick to Sydney, and with the way his jaw is twitching, I'm lucky he doesn't raise his voice at her. In my current mood, I'd probably try to take a chunk out of him, and while I'm younger, there's no doubt that Iron-Shin Seth Isles could school me in what it means to be an MMA fighter.

"I'm sorry. I had to take care of a few things," I answer evenly. "I'm sure Dad mentioned it to you." In the corner, Dad meets my gaze and nods. "I'm here now. Let's get on with it."

Seth advances on me, hands fisted at his sides, arms like twin pythons ready to strike. "You don't get to decide when we get on with something, Gabe. That's my job. Lucky for you, we've still got time to wrap your hands and warm you up before you're due in the cage." He jerks his head toward a chair. "Sit." To Sydney, he says, "Lena is in the second row from the front. She saved you a seat."

She nods and takes off, accustomed to his brusqueness at times like this. Meanwhile, I sit, meek as a kitten, and wait while he straddles a chair opposite and gets to work on my hands. We don't speak, the air thick with tension. When he's done with my right hand, he finally breaks the silence.

"Leo is a hard-hitter," he says, so low I have to strain

to hear him. The fact he's talking about the fight bodes well. Maybe he'll forgive me after this. Me in the Ruby Knuckles is a big deal for him, and I nearly cocked it up. "I want you guarding your jaw at all times or you'll leave yourself open for a knockout. He's going to come in heavy with the hands, so we're going to go the opposite route. For every punch he throws, you kick him. Got it? Aim for the body if you can, but legs will do in a pinch. If you don't have room for a kick, throw a knee. Take him apart bit by bit, and whatever the fuck you do, don't let him get you on the ground in a position where he can strike your head. He's as strong as you are, so if you go down, you'd better be sure you can get him where you want him. There's no out-muscling this guy."

I nod, taking the instructions on board. I've watched enough of Leo's fights to know he favors his fists, and rightly so. They're deadly. Most of his wins have been by knockout, but here's the thing: in order to knock someone out, you have to land some punches. I don't intend to give him that chance. Impatience seethes within me, consuming me. I'm ready to get out there and do some damage, so Sydney and I can pick up where we left off.

Seth releases my hands. "After the rubdown, you can warm up and Jase will spar with you."

He gestures to a thick towel on the floor, which I lie on while a physio rubs liniment over my skin. The liniment has a tangy scent that's sharp every time I inhale, and it works into my muscles more deeply, warming them. He spreads the liniment over all of my exposed skin, excluding my face, and finishes with my arms, grooving his thumbs into the meaty parts. Finally, feeling loose and disturbingly languid considering what's about to come, I get up and run on the spot. My steps are light, and I stay on the balls of my feet. A few minutes pass, and no one says anything. Even Devon is unusually circumspect.

Once I'm in a good headspace, I do a few stretches and then shove my hands into a pair of heavily padded boxing gloves—chosen to ensure Jase and I don't injure each other before I enter the cage. We touch gloves, then move into our stances. Usually when sparring, Jase's tactic is to bring people to the floor, but he won't do that now—it's too risky—which is why I'm partnered with him and not loose cannon Devon.

He launches a tentative attack, coming at me with a quick jab and a kick that would land lightly on my thigh, but I check it with a shin and respond with a push kick to his gut. He tries the arcing right-handed punch that Leo is known for, and I slip out of the way and thrust my knee into his midsection. The air leaves his lungs on a whoomph and I take advantage of his pause to grab his head and drill my knee toward it, stopping short but leaving no doubt as to the damage I could have inflicted. I let him go and he cracks his neck and sucks in a few breaths, then we continue, with him taking the offensive and me countering until Seth calls an end to it. When I've been cleared by the medic, I take a quick drink, put my mouthguard in, and shrug into the Crown MMA fight jacket.

Dad comes over and sets his hands on my shoulders. His eyes shine with emotion, and he squeezes affectionately. "I'm proud of you, *mijo*." His voice is rough. "You're a good man, and I'm sorry if I've been hard on you lately. Go out there and give it your all. Whatever happens, your *mama* and I love you so much."

My throat thickens, and I swallow. Now isn't the time to get emotional. "Thanks, *Papa*. Love you, too."

He gives me one final squeeze, then moves away. The wait for someone to collect us is brief. A guy sticks his head around the door and gestures for us to follow. I take the lead, Seth behind me, followed by Jase and then Devon. At our gym, the fighter always steps foot in the stadium first because it gets the crowd pumped. The coach has their back, and the other corners come in order of seniority. There's nothing random about our pre-fight rituals.

Death metal shrieks over the speakers, and adrenaline spikes in my veins as I stride into the massive space and the audience roars their approval. The crowd is intense tonight because our match has been hyped in the media for weeks. Two prodigal sons of MMA, engaging in a full-scale war. A lot of money will have changed hands. I try to ignore that. To drown out the screams and focus on the rapid-fire beat of my song. Fists wave in the air and people chant my name as I pace the length of the catwalk. My eyes automatically seek Sydney in the second row from the front, and she screams support. I hear her, clear as day, above every other voice.

Get in, bust heads, claim my girl.

When I reach the octagon, I bare my teeth for the umpire, to show my mouthguard, and he grips my fists, checking my gloves haven't been tampered with. Then he nods, and I step up into the cage.

The song switches and the crowd turns toward the entrance, waiting for Leo to emerge. I walk the perimeter of the ring, ignoring both the audience and my opponent until he reaches the umpire, at which time I return to my rightful spot and meet his eyes as he enters. He nods, and I tilt my head, too. We may be opposing forces tonight, but I have a lot of respect for the guy, and he seems to feel the same way about me.

We're called into the center, where the umpire gives us the standard set of instructions and disclaimers, then we each back off. Every one of my nerves is on a knife's edge, waiting for the timer to begin. I scrape a foot over the mats, making sure my grip is solid. From here, I can see the shininess of Leo's forehead and the determined squareness of his jaw. I can't read anything in his expression, but then, I wouldn't expect to. He's too experienced to give anything away, just like I am.

The timer sounds, and I move. While I prefer to counter rather than stage a frontal attack, I'm also not going to stay in place and let him corner me against the wire. Leo is clever enough not to mistake my actions for weakness and rush in, as a less seasoned fighter may do. Instead, he probes at the edge of my defenses, feeling me out, throwing jabs that fall short just to see what I'll do about it.

A hush has descended over the stadium, everyone laser-focused on us. I watch every movement he makes. After weeks of studying his fights in YouTube clips, I've accustomed myself to his micro-gestures and trained myself to recognize them. When his rhythm is perfectly fluid, he's playing it by ear, but right now he has a strategy, and every time his back leg lifts, he hesitates slightly before putting it back down. He's looking for the perfect opportunity to come at me with a kick.

Usually, I don't mind the uncharacteristic slowness of my fights, but Sydney flashes into my head and I want this over so I can get to her. Analyzing the situation, the fastest way to do that seems to be to let him play out whatever combination of strikes he's planned and then do what I do best: counter. If he's going to kick, my best bet is to take advantage of that. Seth's warning about not taking him down unless I'm sure I can finish it pops into my head but I shake it off. I'm feeling good about this.

Lunging forward, I aim a jab and a cross at his face. In return, his sturdy shin slams into my ribs, exactly as I expected it to. The impact sends a violent shockwave through me, but it's a small price to pay to get the upper hand. Because despite all appearances to the contrary, I do have the upper hand. Before his foot can drop, I knock the grounded leg out from under him and he hits the floor with a thud, landing hard on his back. He wheezes and tries to right himself, but I'm already on him, pummeling his face. He tries to roll, but there's no escaping me in this position. Instead, he curls in on himself as much as possible, shielding his head with his arms.

He doesn't give up. He shifts his weight, doing his best to dislodge me, and eventually, it works. Scrambling away from him, I leap to my feet and raise my fists. Then, before he has enough time to think through his next step, I push-kick his diaphragm, and while he's off-balance, I deliver the final blow: a flying knee to the face. Blood spurts from his nose but he doesn't clutch at it. Instead, he drops like a rock.

Knockout.

In a career spanning years, I've had very few knockouts. It isn't how I prefer to roll. But this time, I'm just glad the fight is at an end. Medics rush to Leo's side and after a few seconds, he rouses. They help him up, but it's all over. There's no way he can continue. After conferring briefly, the judges make it official, and the umpire summons us to his side. Leo's coach supports him while the umpire raises my hand. Next thing I know, a video camera is being shoved in my face and some guy in a suit is asking me questions. I answer in a daze, vaguely aware that this is something I've been working toward for years, and yet the victory feels unsatisfying. I guess I assumed that I'd be happy once I did what I've trained for, but instead, I just feel flat.

Pleased, yes. Grateful that I can give Dad something he's always wanted. But not happy.

No, what makes me happy has big brown eyes, brown skin, and soft curves a guy could get lost in. She's my best friend and my lover. If I have anything to say about it, she'll stay that way.

22

Cameras are thrust into Gabe's face, and people vie for his attention. Meanwhile, I'm still trying to convince my brain to accept what it just witnessed. Yes, Gabe can be brutal. He has to be, in his line of work. But I've never seen him take down anyone like that before. Leo didn't stand a chance. And now, everyone is rallying around him, desperate to congratulate him on his success, and he just looks dazed and bemused, like he hasn't quite come to terms with it himself yet.

His gaze lands on me, and focuses in. Tentatively, I smile. Then someone says something to him, and he turns away. His body is still tense, because his brain hasn't accepted that the fight is over. Mentally, he's poised to strike. I'm not surprised, because he's been training for this for so long and has built it up in his mind so much that he can't comprehend it ending so quickly.

Brutal. Calculating. Efficient. That's my Gabe in the cage.

As his eyes find mine again, something other than

detachment finally flickers in them, and my stomach flutters in response. A man speaks to him, but he doesn't take his eyes from me. Suddenly, there's a microphone in his hand and his voice booms around the stadium.

"Thanks everyone," he says, still staring at me. "I appreciate your support. I'm so grateful to have had this opportunity and to be able to stand here tonight as your Ruby Knuckles champion." The crowd roars, and he waits for them to quiet before continuing. His eyes flick away from me, toward Leo, who's standing in the corner, out of the spotlight. "Great fight, man." Leo nods, and Gabe turns to Tomas. "Many of you know the story of how my dad's professional career ended in the Ruby Knuckles final, but what you might not know is that he went on to become one of the best managers in the business. I'm so proud to stand here tonight as both his son and his student. *Papa*, you taught me everything you know, but the most important thing you gave me was heart."

Tomas swipes at the bottoms of his eyes, which are suspiciously moist. I wish I could hug them both. This is such a huge moment for them. The culmination of everything they've worked for.

"And that's why I'm taking a three-month break."

Silence descends in a rush. I could hear a pin drop. No one dares to say a thing. Meanwhile, I'm trying to figure out what on earth is going on in Gabe's head. Seth's shocked expression tells me this is news to him, too. "Vacation" is not a word in Gabe's vocabulary.

"I'm following my heart," he says, as though that explains everything. "You see, there's this girl, and she's been waiting for me forever. I think it's about time I do a little waiting on her."

Oh, my God. *Oh, my God.*

Lena bumps me with her elbow. "Did you know about this?"

Mutely, I shake my head. In the cage, Gabe hands off the microphone and strides to the edge, then leaps out, heading my way. He's built like a bear, but moves like a panther, all sleek muscles and fluid motion.

My fighting panther. Burning me up with his gaze.

He stops in front of me, and Lena shoves my shoulder.

"Go," she hisses.

I stand on shaking legs. Gabe offers me a hand and I take it, grateful for the physical support. He's still wearing his gloves, and they're damp with perspiration, but I hardly notice because suddenly everyone's attention is on me. I can practically see the questions in their eyes. Without saying a single thing, he escorts me out the same way he came in. People cheer as he passes, and many reach their hands out. He bumps fists with a couple of guys but doesn't release me, and based on how tightly he's holding on, he doesn't plan to. As soon as we're out of view, he drags me into an empty side room and pivots to face me.

"We can talk now," he says, the strain audible in his voice. "I did the fight, and now it's just you and me. That was the deal."

I nod, because I don't trust myself to speak after his big announcement. Especially when he's so close and emitting all of those damn pheromones that men give off after they've been sweating. It's very Neanderthal of me, but watching Gabe physically best another man has my entire body eager for his touch.

"What are you doing?" I ask. "You can't just take a sabbatical without any warning."

"Yeah." One side of his mouth hitches up. "I kinda can."

"But why?" It doesn't make any sense to me. All I know is that everything is changing, and not in the way I expected.

"For us. I know I haven't always been good to you in the past," he says slowly, and the squeeze of his fingers around mine reminds me that he's holding my hand. "I've brushed you off or forgotten our plans because of other things going on in my life. I regret that, but I can't go back and change it."

I cling to his hand, waiting to see where he's going with this.

"The last few weeks have been messy as hell—all those emotional highs and lows—but they really helped me get my shit in order." He steps closer, and now he's so near me that when my nipples peak, they almost touch his glistening chest. "You're my priority, Syd. From here on out."

God, I hope he can't feel my hand quivering. Everything inside me is vibrating like crazy. I want to believe him so badly.

"What does that mean?"

He dips his head and his breath tickles my hairline. "It means that I'm all yours for the next three months."

"But how—"

He stops me with a look. "I'll obviously need to keep in shape—although I'm going to rest plenty too. I'll sort the details out with *Papa* later, but it's happening. I need to slow down a bit. Learn to take it easy. My mental game has been all over the place, and I need to get myself together and be clear about what actually matters. I want to date you properly, and take you on that beachside vacation you've always dreamed of." His lips curl, and his smile is so breathtak-ingly hopeful I can hardly stand it. "My job is never going to be normal, babe, but I want you more than anything else, and from now on, I promise you'll always come first."

He's saying everything I've always wished to hear, but is it just words? Or will he follow them up with action?

"But then what?" I ask. "After your vacation, is every-thing supposed to magically resolve itself? Because the real world doesn't work that way."

"No, it doesn't," he allows. "But the time away will give me a chance to figure out how to readjust. I'll talk to Jase and other guys on the circuit, and work out how they balance their personal and work lives. You and I can come up with a plan together. Even if I only fight a couple of times a year, I can earn enough money from that and endorsements to provide us with everything we need. Most of my winnings so far are invested anyway, so I could survive for years without working if I needed to."

"But you shouldn't," I protest. "You love what you do."

"I never said I'd stop. But I can slow down." His expression becomes wry. "The fact is, I love training and being with my team, but I don't need to fight as often as I do in order to have a good career." His free hand curves around the side of my face, and a shiver slides down my spine. "I want to make time for us, if you'll have me."

Staring deep into his dark eyes, I can tell he means it. He really, truly does. With that, the last of my insecu-rities and uncertainties lift from my shoulders and fly away.

"Yes," I whisper, going up onto my toes. "I will. I love

you, Gabe."

His smile is slow and soft. "I was worried I'd never hear that from you." He drops a kiss on my lips. "I love you too, Syd. *Te amo.* So goddamned much."

He kisses me again, and again, each deeper than the one before, and then his hands journey down to my butt and he's taking my weight as I wrap my legs around his waist. Backing me into the wall, he nuzzles at my throat.

"I promise to be the guy you deserve from now on. Come home with me today?"

I clasp him tight, my heart welling over with affection for the man who's both my lover and my best friend. "Will you drive me to work on your motorcycle tomorrow?"

"I'll take you anywhere you want. On one condition." Drawing back, he meets my eyes. "Me and my bike are the only things that go between your thighs from now on."

A laugh bursts from me, and I shake my head, grinning. "Of course, you silly man." His eyes light up and then darken as I grind against him. "Now take me home, and show me what you're made of." To my surprise, he starts toward the exit, still holding me. I swat his shoulder. "Put me down!"

"No." He palms my ass. "I'm finally having my moment. Remember when Jase carried Lena out of here after his championship fight?"

"Yeah." I'm not sure where this is going.

"I wanted to do the same to you," he confesses. "And now I finally get to. Let me have my moment."

"Okay." Relaxing into his arms, I rest my head on his shoulder. It's a miracle he can even walk with me in this position. We pass a number of people who look curiously over their shoulders. I don't care. I'm too happy to care.

"As far as I'm concerned, we're going to have a lot more moments, so don't go thinking this will be the only one," I caution.

"I wouldn't have it any other way, *mi amor*."

EPILOGUE

DEVON

It's eight a.m. the Sunday following Gabe's epic fight and I arrive at the gym, as per usual. Where else would I be on a Sunday morning? I spend more time in this place than I do in my own home. Although to be fair, if my place was as nice as Jase's or Gabe's, I might spend more time there. As it is, I haven't proven myself as much as they have, which means I've won less money, have fewer sponsorships, and spend my nights in a nice apartment only a few blocks from here rather than in a mansion.

Pushing the door open, I step inside, expecting the place to be empty. Seth's been sleeping in his office lately—I'm not even sure if he has an apartment anymore—but he usually doesn't rise until late morning on the day after an event. Curiously, he's in the octagon at the end of the gym, sparring with someone I haven't seen before. I blink as my eyes adjust to the light. Seth's sparring partner is average height, lean, and light on their feet. As he throws a punch, his partner pivots away, hair whipping in an arc.

Wait—hair?

Removing my shoes, I edge closer to get a better look. The stranger has toned muscles, small breasts, and a mouthwateringly firm ass. It's a woman. The hottest, fiercest woman I've seen. Her face is a mask of concentration. Hazel eyes, strawberry blonde hair that's tied back, and perfect golden skin, like she's spent a lot of time in the sun.

She's wearing boxing gloves and elbow pads, as is Seth, and they're sparring muay thai style, with only stand-up striking. As I watch, spellbound, she practically dances across the mat in graceful movements that end with a fake and the solid delivery of a knee just below the center of his ribs. But that damage isn't enough for this warrior princess. She follows it up with an elbow to his face, in the perfect place to split the skin if her arms weren't padded. The timer beeps shrilly, ending their round, and she bumps fists with Seth, the edges of her mouth lifting, her cheeks flushed with triumph.

Oh, fuck. I'm a goner.

This girl is fucking glorious.

My strides eat up the distance to the octagon.

"Hey, Seth," I call. "Who's the newbie?"

Her smile twists into a scowl and hell if that doesn't make me crazier about her. She's got wildness in her, the same as me.

"Dev." He glances at the clock. "Weren't expecting you yet." He jumps down, then turns and waits for her to follow. "I guess now is as good a time as any."

It isn't until they're standing side by side in front of me that discomfort worms its way into my gut. Seth and this beautiful woman—the new owner of my heart—

have exactly the same shade of hair, and identical stand-offish expressions.

Oh, shit. Surely not.

"This is my sister, Harley," he tells me, slinging an arm around her shoulders.

Oh, hell. *No.*

My stomach hits the floor. I have the worst luck ever. My muay thai princess is Seth's baby sister? That makes things a whole lot more complicated.

"Harley," he continues, eyes narrowing in a way that says he knows what's going on in my head. "This is Devon Green. One of my fighters."

"Hi," she says, and extends a gloved hand for me to bump. Even her voice is sexy. It's husky, like she doesn't use it often.

"Hey, Harley." Love her name. It matches her perfectly. I want to say it aloud as often as possible.

"Dev, Harley has just moved back from Thailand. I wasn't planning to make an announcement until tomorrow, but she's competing in an eight-woman elimination tournament in a couple of months. I want to broaden our horizons and get more women competing through the gym. Harley is going to be our drawcard. If she wins, we'll make a name for ourselves as a good place for women to train."

"Wow, that's crazy cool." I look at her with increased respect. "Eight-woman eliminator. Intense."

She grins, and it blows me away. My knees nearly knock together. "I'm ready for it."

"Almost," Seth amends, his gaze full of affection when it lands on her. "But her experience is solely in kickboxing and muay thai, which means she needs to learn how to grapple, and fast. She'll be training with you boys—Jase, especially. She's a quick study."

I nod. "Welcome aboard, Harley. We're all like family around here."

"Exactly." Seth's eyes narrow further, and an icy finger traces down my spine. "Like *family*," he repeats. "So don't get any ideas about anything you wouldn't do with your brothers, Dev."

And there it is. He's officially telling me: Harley Isles is off-limits.

You know what?

That only makes me want her more.

EXTENDED EPILOGUE

Gabe—three years later

"It never gets any less gorgeous," Sydney says as she walks ahead of me, exiting our cabin in Provincetown on Cape Cod, and stepping onto the beach. We've been coming here each summer since we got together and love it so much that we decided to buy a cottage by the water.

We're both barefoot because the sand is soft and the summer weather is better than I could have dreamed. It's warm, and there's a hum of anticipation in the air. Despite that, the beach is largely empty. Most of the tourists are at the fair in town, which is why I chose today for this very important lunch date. Nerves thrum through my entire body, and I'm so wired that it's lucky Sydney hasn't figured out what I'm up to.

She waits for me to reach her side, then threads her fingers through mine, locking our palms together. Sparks of awareness zing between us at the contact, and she smiles, the expression extending all the way to her eyes, which crinkle at the corners. The breeze stirs the loose strands of hair curling around her face, and I brush them aside, letting my touch linger on her skin.

God, I love her.

I love her massive heart and her generous personality. I love those deep brown eyes and I really fucking love getting my hands all over her.

We wander along the beach, side by side, then veer toward the water. Midway, we stop, and I place the picnic basket in my other hand on the ground. Inside is a blanket, which I spread on the sand for us to sit on. Dropping to my knees, I sneak a glance at her bronze legs beneath the hem of her sundress, and then unpack a bottle of chilled sparkling grape juice and a selection of gourmet finger foods—cheeses, dried fruit, olives, tomatoes, and some fancy cracker things that look a bit weird but taste great. There's also a small box of artisan chocolates I picked up from a shop downtown, and I pass them to her.

"Oh, these look good," she says as she removes the lid. She chooses one and pops it into her mouth. Her eyes close and she moans in bliss.

Instantly, I'm hard. Constant erections are the only drawback of being around her. Even after the years we've been together, she can still set me off with one small sound. When she swallows, I lean over and kiss her, my tongue delving into her mouth, tasting chocolate and Sydney. So. Damn. Good. I'm a greedy bastard when it comes to her.

Don't get carried away.

I brought her out here to propose, not to fuck her on the beach, in plain view of anyone who happens along. Backing off, I collect a pair of paper cups and half-fill each with grape juice—I'm due for a fight in a few weeks, so I'm off alcohol. I pass one to Sydney and we toast each other. She takes a sip, then sets her cup aside and reaches for a cracker. Meanwhile, the box in the pocket of my board shorts is burning a hole into my thigh. My mouth is parched and I gulp the juice, which fizzes up the back of my nose.

Mustering my courage, I shift around so I'm kneeling in front of her, and stick my hand into my pocket. My fingers fumble with the box, but I extract it and manage to get it open. Her eyes widen and she sits up straight.

"Sydney," I say, the speech I rehearsed promptly vanishing from my mind. Instead, I speak from the heart, and my words are not elaborate but they're true. "I love you. I'm crazy for you. You're the most important part of my life, and I hope you know that."

She nods, her eyes sparkling with emotion.

"Marry me?"

"Yes," she breathes, ignoring the ring in favor of kissing me—which, hey, I'm all good with. My heart is still trying to beat its way out of my chest, and she smooths a hand over it. "Your pulse is going wild."

"I was nervous," I admit, even though it isn't very manly. "You're this amazing, talented, beautiful surgeon, and I'm just a guy who can take a punch and keep on swinging."

She shakes her head. "You're so much more than that. You're the man who's made me happier than ever over the past three years. Of course I want to marry you." Her lips curl up, and she presses a soft kiss to my forehead. "Now, let's see this ring."

I slide the ring from its resting place and onto her finger. It fits, because I learned from Jase's example and asked Lena to figure out her size. It isn't flashy or chunky, because if it was she wouldn't be able to wear it at work. It's a simple gold band inlaid with small, glittering diamonds.

"Do you like it?" I ask, suddenly afraid that opting for functionality may not have been the best idea.

"Are you kidding?" Her grin widens. "It's absolutely perfect. Thank you. Actually," something flickers in her expression, "I have my own news I wanted to share with you today."

Instantly, my gaze darts to her stomach. It looks the same as usual, but I can tell from the excitement gleaming in her eyes that I'm going to like what she's about to say.

"I did a test this morning to confirm, but I wanted to wait until the perfect moment to tell you... we're having a baby, Gabe."

Reaching over, I haul her into my arms and kiss her senseless. While we haven't been actively trying to get pregnant, she stopped taking the pill a while ago because we've both talked about how much we want a family. Sydney, especially, wants to be a mother. She has so much love to give, and unlike with her mom, it isn't conditional.

"That's fucking amazing," I tell her when I draw back. My hand goes to her belly and caresses it through her dress. It's hard to believe that there's a whole other person in there—one who's half her and half me, the most pure expression of our love. "I can't wait to meet the little guy."

"Or girl." Her lips quirk. "You're going to be an amazing dad. Our child will be lucky to have you."

My heart lifts. What did I do to deserve this wonderful woman?

"I love you, *mi vida*."

"I love you, too," she says, and then pushes me onto

my back on the blanket and straddles me. "This calls for a celebration."

Hell, yes.

Every day of the rest of my life will be a celebration with her by my side.

That's why I'm going to keep her.

My lover, my best friend, my girl.

Forever.

THE END

FIGHTER'S SECRET EXCERPT

Harley

I dodge a punch my half-brother throws at me and wish it was this easy to evade the blows life keeps dealing me lately. Seth is twice my size, but also twelve years older and out of practice. Yeah, he might spar with the fighters who train here at Crown MMA Gym—one of Las Vegas's premier homes of professional mixed martial arts—but he hasn't fought in ages. Meanwhile, I've been living and breathing muay thai for years, and it shows.

Here in the cage, I have it all together. I can forget about the way my world has crumbled around me and simply exist in the moment. In fact, it's essential to do so because if I slip out of the present, I might find myself eating one of Seth's famous straight rights. I smirk as I circle him, looking for a weak point, loving the challenge. Most people don't understand my passion for fighting. It's not a typical occupation for a twenty-something woman.

With a quick, practiced motion, I strike, snapping my padded shin out to thud into the inner part of his thigh. He's slow to react, and his leg starts to buckle beneath him. Knowing he'll save himself before he hits the floor, I use his distraction against him and ram my knee into his solar plexus.

Bam. Got you.

He recovers before I can take a shot at his head, and wrestles me into a clinch. His arms are like anacondas, so there's no way I can overpower him, which means I need to either bear it out, or outsmart him.

God, I love this—even when I get a noseful of his sweat-soaked shoulder. I haven't sparred with Seth since he was a UFC champion. I've been out of the country for years, but the time apart hasn't changed how it feels to let loose with him like this. It's the way we communicate. The only language we're both fluent in. And now that I'm here, with his support, I'm beginning to feel like the sun is rising on a new day and perhaps everything will turn out all right.

"Lock me up," he grunts, ever the coach.

Maneuvering him into the corner, I wind my leg around his so he can't do anything, and hold on. When the timer shrieks, ending the round, I release him. We bump fists, then I yank one of my gloves off, grab a towel from where it's hanging over the edge of the cage, and mop my face with it. My hair is coming loose, so I wrangle it back into a ponytail.

"You're good," Seth says, his lips pursing as he evaluates me. I wonder what he sees: the baby sister I used to be, or the athlete Thailand turned me into. "But we need to get you grappling sooner rather than later if you're going to win that eight-man eliminator."

I nod, acknowledging what we both know: I'm at a significant disadvantage for my big debut. He's signed me up for my first professional MMA bouts—three in one night. Eight women begin the tournament, and only one emerges as victor. We both want me to be the one left standing, even if our reasons for that differ. He wants the good publicity it'll bring his gym, while I need a win after the month I've had.

The trouble is, all of my professional experience is in muay thai, which is strictly stand-up striking. MMA, with the jiu-jitsu element on the floor, is a completely different beast. That's okay, though. I'm ready for it. I have nothing but time on my hands to prepare. I uprooted my entire life to move back here, and I don't even have a bed to call my own. Seth is loaning me his spare room, but to be honest, I'm not sure how often I'll sleep there. After living on-site at my gym in Thailand, it'll be hard to move into an apartment. I already miss the sun and warmth. Unfortunately, I couldn't stay. Not after what happened.

"Do five rounds on bags, then we'll talk through your training plan."

With that, I'm dismissed. I slip my glove back on and head to one of the heavy bags. After a moment, I feel eyes on my back and turn to find an insanely hot fighter watching me.

Devon.

Even his name is sexy. He sends me a wicked grin, then strips off his shirt and starts punching a bag. His brown abs glisten with sweat and shift beneath his skin like he's a sleek panther. But men with abs are nothing new to me, and however yummy he is, he looks like trouble. I don't need any more of that right now. Besides, Seth warned me before I even set foot in the gym, not to hook up with any of his fighters—something about not introducing unnecessary drama—and I know he's made it clear to them that I'm off-limits too.

Turning back to the bag, I take a moment to scope out its size and shape. It's newer than the ones I'm used to. Flashier too. Getting into stance, I throw a jab then a cross, and snap my fists back to my chin. *Always protect the jaw.* Trust me, I learned that lesson fast. I reach out to get a sense of the distance, then back off and slam a kick into it. My shin thumps across the solid fabric, but I hardly feel it. Bags are nothing compared to the dozens of shins that have clashed with my own.

Now that I'm comfortable with the bag, I launch a few combinations. Punches, kicks, knees, elbows. Shortly, the beeper ends the round. I drop to the floor and start doing sit-ups. Not that I have to. The thirty seconds between rounds is technically a break, but I like to make the most of the time I've got.

A face appears above me. Dark eyes and a mischievous smile. I continue my sit-ups, ignoring the way my body reacts to the handsome fighter, tingling in places it shouldn't. I silently reprimand it. A nice smile and a killer physique don't make a man worth my time. Recent experience should tell me that.

"Good form," he says, raking his gaze down my body in a way that brings my nipples to attention. Fortunately, it's impossible to see anything through my thick sports bra.

"Thanks. I try."

He winks. "You succeed."

Oh, my God. He's a flirt. Exactly what I don't need.

The beeper ends the break, and Devon offers me a hand up. I grab it and haul myself to my feet. But something strange happens when we touch. Energy pulses through my body, awakening every nerve until I'm hyperaware of the movement of my skin against his. The instant my feet are steady beneath me, I drop his hand, desperate to end the strange sensation. His eyes catch mine and the way he searches them tells me he felt it too, but far from being discomfited, he seems enthralled. He doesn't return to his bag as I expect. Instead, he wraps an arm around mine, effectively taking it out of commission.

"So how are you settling into Vegas?"

I shrug, irritated with him for getting up in my face with all of his sexiness. "It's fine. It's no Thailand, but there are worse places."

"I bet Seth hasn't given you the grand tour." He cocks his head, and his full lips twitch into a smile. Something twinges inside of me, and I have the insane urge to bite into his lower lip. Shaking my head, I clear the thought. "I'm an excellent tour guide," he continues, "and I happen to be free as soon as training ends. I'll show you around."

"No, thanks. I'm perfectly capable of figuring the city out for myself."

His brows shoot up. "Oh, so that's how you're going to play it?"

"Play what?"

"You're going to pretend you don't feel this thing between us?"

I shake my head, incredulous. "We just met."

He shrugs. "That doesn't mean anything. Some of the world's greatest romances happened in only a few days."

This guy really is trouble. "Didn't Seth give you 'the talk'?"

His grin widens. "I offered to show you around town, that's all. I'd do the same for any other fighter who was new to the area."

"Uh-huh." I glance at the timer and see he's already

wasted half of the round. "Listen, I haven't worked out for several days because I've been in transit and I really need to get back into it. Do you mind?"

He releases the bag, but I can tell from his expression that this isn't the end of the conversation. He might be backing off for now, but it's a temporary reprieve. That's fine. I look forward to round two.

"Dev!" Seth yells across the room. "Harley! Less talking, more sparring."

"Me and her?" His smile falters, but he catches it quickly. He wasn't expecting that.

"Come on, then." I raise my fists and challenge him, waiting to see what he'll do. Some guys don't like sparring with a female partner. They get weird about it.

He bumps my gloves and steps back, scanning me in a way that's two-thirds analytical and one-third sexual. He's trying to take me seriously, but can't help checking me out. I resist the urge to roll my eyes. That's such a guy thing to do, and honestly, I hope he underestimates me. Silently, I dare him to.

He moves forward, but he's hesitant and all it takes is a push-kick in the solar plexus to stop him in his tracks. He fires back with a body kick but it's slow and weak. I check it easily and sigh. So this is how it's going to be. He's afraid to hurt me. As if he really could. I'm not some delicate flower, and by the time this round is over, he'll know not to treat me like one.

He throws a half-hearted hook, which I block, and then I step forward and deliver a perfectly placed uppercut to the soft piece of flesh on the underside of his chin. His eyes bulge in shock, but rather than looking annoyed as most men typically do when they're outdone by a woman, he laughs and studies me like I'm the most fascinating thing he's ever seen.

Devon

So this is how it feels to be punched in the face by love. I have to say, I kind of like it. I like this girl, too. She's a warrior princess who put Seth on his ass and turned down my invitation without a second thought. Harley Isles isn't going to be easy to win over, but the worthwhile adventures never are. All I know for sure is that I can't wait to learn more about her. To find out what gets under her skin.

Moving forward, I keep my guard up because she packs a lot of power for her size, and clearly has the skills to take down a guy like me if I don't stay on my toes. I fucking love that about her. This time, I throw a fake with my left arm, then as she shields her face, I drop low and land a shot to her gut. Or perhaps I should say her abs, because there's nothing soft about them. They flex beneath my fist and the air gusts from her lungs, but she doesn't crumple or gasp for breath. Instead, she seizes the opportunity to strike while my head is low, aiming her knee at my face. It's only my catlike reflexes that save me from a bleeding nose.

"You're good," I say around my mouthguard.

She rolls her eyes. "I've literally lived at a gym for eight years. What'd you expect?"

"Eight years?" I can hardly fathom it. She looks around the same age as me, perhaps a year or two older, so she must have only been a teenager when she left the country. Perhaps she found her way to the martial arts younger than I did. I was an aimless kid. The guy everyone liked, but who never really belonged. At least, not until I found MMA.

She jabs, and I slip the punch and haul her into a

clinch. Her body presses against mine from thigh to chest, and it's the best sensation short of sex that I've ever experienced. The places where we touch are practically alight with the flames of attraction. With one leg, I try to sweep her to the floor, but she evades the movement and counters by rolling me over her hip. Her actions are less practiced than they have been until now, and I realize that's because she's not familiar with ground play. Throwing and wrestling are off the cards in muay thai.

A devilish grin steals across my face. Suddenly, there's nothing I want more than to get her on the floor, where she's at a disadvantage, just to see what she'll do. If I trap her in a hold, will she tap out? I doubt it. She's the type to be stubborn until she's blue in the face. As if she senses the direction of my thoughts, she shoves me away.

"You don't like getting up close and personal," I say.

She scowls. "Not true."

"Oh, so you want to get close to me?" I waggle my eyebrows, watching as her jaw tightens.

Instead of answering, she kicks the side of my body, then slams her padded shin into my thigh. Because I'm distracted, I'm too slow to check the kicks and if this fight were for real, she'd have scored a couple of clean points. She knows it, too. Her expression is smug, and I can't lie, her desire to prove she can beat the crap out of me is sexy as hell.

I launch into one of my favorite combos, curious how she'll react. She responds fluidly and within seconds, I find myself engaged in a dangerous dance. Sparring is one of my favorite pastimes, and she seems to feel the same because our bodies speak to each other as we move, and they're far more honest than our mouths. It's playful, but no longer tentative. We're learning each other's limitations and preferences. Our patterns and habits.

Yeah, I know. Sounds like sex.

Well, guess what? Sparring and sex have a lot in common. They're both weirdly intimate, and you have to trust a good sparring partner almost as much as you'd trust a sexual partner. After all, one false move and you eat a fist.

Seth approaches and starts barking instructions. They're directed at Harley so I tune them out, trying to figure out what throws her off her game. I'm unpredictable. That's my major tactic. I thrive on shocking people and then pressing my advantage, but Harley is unflappable in the face of my strategy, calmly returning blows and moving as though there's music only she can hear. For five rounds, we continue, with Seth drilling her during the breaks. *Try this. Do that. Don't let him get in your head.* I have to admit, I like the thought of being in her head. I want her thinking about me. Preferably wondering what's beneath my clothes. Not that she appears to be doing so, damn it all.

When we're done, I grab my drink bottle and towel, and wipe the sweat from my brow. Seth heads into his office, leaving me and Harley alone in the training area. A perfect opportunity.

Sidling over to her, I lower my voice and say, "Pretty sure you're my soul mate, Harls. Come zip-lining with me. It'll be fun."

She rolls her gorgeous hazel eyes. "You're being ridiculous."

"What?" I act shocked. "You don't want to be my soul mate?"

She flushes. Even though she's tanned—probably

from training in the sun—her complexion is naturally fair and does nothing to hide the pinkness blossoming in her cheeks. It's fucking adorable. If I said that, she'd castrate me, but it's true. It also shows that she's not immune to the strange pull I'm feeling, she's just doing her best to pretend it isn't happening.

"You heard what Seth said," she grumbles, and looks away under the guise of reaching for her water.

"I did," I agree. "But as much as I respect him, my coach doesn't dictate my personal life, so as far as I'm concerned, that doesn't mean shit." Besides, Seth is my friend. He might be pissy if I date his sister at first, but once he sees I'm serious about her, it won't be a problem. "If you're not attracted to me—if you don't feel this tension between us—then come straight out and say it, and I'll leave you alone." Searching her eyes, I pray she doesn't pull the lever on the escape hatch I offered.

Her eyes narrow, but she shakes her head. "I can't do that."

Then she turns and stalks away, her ponytail swaying down the center of her back. I gulp. Round one to me. She's interested. I just need to work harder to woo her.

ALSO BY A. RIVERS

ACKNOWLEDGMENTS

This book couldn't have happened without the support of my favorite person ever. AKA Mr. R. AKA Hubby. AKA Reluctant Dog Daddy. You're my rock. I love the hell out of you.

Some others who need acknowledgement are the girls who used to train alongside me every day. Leysa, Jess, Asher, and Kaitlyn, you are the toughest women I've known and I grew so much from spending time with you. Also, you may have inspired a character in the next book. Wait and see.

To Sheridan, Evie, Laura, Leticia, and Renita, thanks so much for your feedback—it made such a difference. I ended up adding a whole other character and 10,000 words to give depth to the story. Thanks to Serena, for asking the practical questions such as 'Are you sure these body parts align?', and for always making me a better writer and building me up. Thank you to Kate, you are such a joy to work with. Lastly, thanks to Maria, for designing the perfect covers for this series. I love you all.

ABOUT THE AUTHOR

A. Rivers writes romance with strong heroes and heroines who kick butt and take names. She loves MMA fighters, investigators, military men, bodyguards, and the protective guy next door who isn't afraid to fight the odds for love.